CALL ME OBIE

Liminal Books

Liminal Books is an imprint of Between the Lines Publishing. The Liminal Books name and logo are trademarks of Between the Lines Publishing.

Cover design by Cherie Fox

Between the Lines Publishing
1769 Lexington Ave N., Ste 286
Roseville, MN 55113
btwnthelines.com

Published: November 2022

Original ISBN (Paperback) 978-1-958901-09-0
Original ISBN (eBook) 978-1-958901-10-6

CALL ME OBIE

Ateret Haselkorn

For my Ronny

Chapter 1

I didn't have to pay for my heart because of The Vote. My parents won't tell me how they voted, but I can imagine my mother, her ankles swollen, one of her hands supporting her pregnant belly, leaning over the digital console to face this decision with full knowledge that I'd be born with blue lips, the need for multiple cardiac surgeries, and a higher risk of learning disabilities. What parents wouldn't want their defective daughter to have an artificial heart three-dimensionally printed for them? Who wouldn't want to hit the reset button on their baby's most important organ with little risk, and for free?

I am a "Mooch," a beneficiary of the Magnanimous Organ Outturn for Child Health program. I think that people knew devices were going to be expensive, the same way that the price of wheelchairs, the good ones, made them out of reach for many back in the day. Guilt made them institute MOOCH so that all of us who were born crappy could rest in the noble arms of society knowing that we were not discriminated

1

against for how we came into this world. I mean, I can't help the way I was born, and most people understand this, or at least say they do before they turn around and vote to lower the age beyond which we're held "responsible" for ourselves.

I think that when the organ donor question was removed from driver's license questionnaires, maybe people stopped feeling like they could help others, maybe they switched from an "ourselves" to a "me and you" point of view. That was when organ printing became common enough to overcome The Scarcity. That's the way history books mention that big gap between the many people who needed organs because they were sick or just didn't want to die yet and all the organs that were available. But, what do I know? I'm fifteen and wasn't alive before the year 2085.

I don't really hate being called a Mooch, though. What I can't stand is the word "artificial." It has to be the most misunderstood modern word of the 22nd Century. The media puts it in front of anything. They started with Intelligence and now it goes with Medicine, Housing, Teaching, and in my case, Organs. When I asked House, the system that runs our home, to look "artificial" up in a thesaurus, I stopped the read-out because I got too irritated. I am not fake. My heart was created for me using my own cells. If that isn't authentic, then I don't know what is.

My best friend Mateo says I overthink things because all "cardio-plants" do; it's as if those ventral cells pump too much blood into our brains. Mateo's cornea was messed up so he's an "eye-plant," or as he likes to say, an *ojoso*. He has to volunteer next to janitorial drones, cleaning up beaches and parks to pay his off because his problems weren't diagnosed until he was older than thirteen.

Mateo can't hide because his transplant went through some kind of spontaneous mutation in the lab that made the tissue adopt a bluish hue instead of being clear. His case was tricky because it required heavy genetic engineering to avoid simply growing a cornea with the same exact issue. The way he tells it, instead of growing another, his parents accepted the defective one for a sharp discount on the number of hours Mateo would have to spend volunteering for it. But Mateo doesn't complain. Actually, he says the best part about his being forced into the open about receiving an artificial organ is that people forget he's Mexican. Just last week he was walking home from school and someone rolled down the window of their vehicle and yelled, "Get an oil change." This, in case you can't tell, is because people think of us as machines.

"See, Obie?" he said to me afterwards, his newer cornea sparkling unevenly. "Humanism trumps racism."

"Is that good?"

"I take pride in making society invent a whole new way to define 'us versus them.' I like to make people really have to think."

Mateo is the only person, aside from my folks, who knows about my heart. He's been my best friend since middle school. The only other thing we have in common, besides being "artificial," is that our parents send us to an old-fashioned, in-person school. Mine do it because they—well, mostly my dad—insist that I spend time in the "real world." He also wants me to have a set schedule instead of the whole on-demand-when-you-feel-like-it approach that Virtual Reality Artificial Intelligence, or VRAI, homeschooling has become. The VRAIs were supposed to be strict but they're also designed to match with our needs and feelings and natural dispositions (the result of another referendum I won't get into). So, my dad, with his hand-knit baggy sweaters that aren't even water resistant, insisted on sending me to a school. The lone one is about a hundred miles away, which only takes fifteen minutes on the speed rail, but is still a pain compared to staying at home in my sweats and VR goggles.

Now, believe me, bullies can figure out how to get to their targets digitally, but I think that having to go to an in-person school delivers us right into the lion's den. That's actually how Mateo and I met, back in the seventh grade. I was gliding along, minding my business in my shiny new hover sneakers—even though I promised my dad that I'd walk for some traditional exercise—when my comm device vibrated with an environmental disturbance alert. It said there was a hazard above me. I looked upwards, scanning the treetops and clouds, and spotted a black, sharp-edged and bird-shaped drone the size of my hand. It flew straight up, reversed direction, and then dove down over and over. As I got closer to it, I heard yelling each time it dropped out of my line of sight. Weird. . . When I got to the school's quad, I saw a thin, golden-skinned boy about my age running around screaming and waving his hands above his head, doing his best to fend off the attack. The hunting drone kept diving to hit him on the forehead with its beak. Every time the boy was down, as in lying on his stomach and moaning, the drone flew up. And whenever the boy shakily stood, it swooped down and jabbed him again. When I reached him, he was resting face down with his bleeding forehead pressed against his forearms.

"Are you okay?" I asked him.

"*Ay, no,*" he replied. Later I'd learn that, as American as Mateo was, his Mexican heritage always emerged when he was under duress. He rolled onto his back and looked up at me. I had one second to take in his one blue and one brown eye before the drone swept in again, jabbing him on the bridge of his nose before he managed to roll back over.

"I think the drone is tracking your eyes," I said as the machine retreated back into the air.

"Wha?" the boy groaned into the artificial grass. His arms were spread before him, and the comm encircling his wrist was cracked.

"When you're face up, it flies in to hurt you. I think it's set to attack your eyes. Mine are both brown and it isn't attacking me."

I think he paused to take this in, or maybe it was the pain that caused his hesitation, who knows?

"So, what do I do?" he finally asked.

"Um . . ." I looked around, as if anything on our carefully landscaped school grounds could possibly help this "real world" situation. The drone silently hovered overhead. "I have an idea," I told him.

"I'm all ears."

I stifled my giggle. His ears did stick out quite a bit and looking at the back of his head made them look really big. I pulled a copy of my dad's retinal scan up on my comm. My dad's eyes are blue (I must have inherited mine from my mom's Chinese and Korean descent), and when I angled my comm a certain way, the sunlight bounced off and a blurry blue reflection landed on the school building wall. The drone didn't budge. It must have been trained to look for blue and brown, a very specific and unique combination. Someone must have really wanted this kid hurt.

I leaned forward and wriggled the cracked comm off the boy's wrist. "Hang on, I have an idea. Just log me into this thing, okay?" Keeping his face down, the boy lifted his head slightly as I held the device below his eyes. It scanned his retina, beeping as it granted access. "Tell it to take a selfie," I said.

"*Amiga*, snap a photo of me," he commanded. I held the comm close to his eye as it carried out the command. It wasn't a retinal scan, but it would be brown and eye shaped, at least. Then I held his comm next to mine, angled them both to catch the sun, and started walking slowly towards the building. The blue and brown circular reflections became smaller the closer I got to the wall, creating a slightly wavy image of mismatched eyes. I held my breath nervously, hoping it would work. Suddenly, there was a whoosh next to my shoulder as the drone zipped past and a loud smash as it crashed into the building and broke apart.

I will give my parents some credit here, in hindsight. They taught me to use my brain before relying on AI.

"Look at the data first! Use your head!" my dad would always say, pacing behind me as I stared at the statistics assignment displayed on my console.

6

"It's the same way I look at my patients," my mom would say, "before the AI tells me what to do."

So, when faced with the weird event of a drone hitting a boy between the eyes whenever his face was turned up, it didn't take much to find a pattern. Then, I mentally listed what resources we had—again, credit to my mother for insisting that I focus on the positive. Finally, we're not really supposed to share retinal scans because of security concerns, but my dad said I could keep a copy of his for emergencies. My own eyes can be used to open our home, get me into our school building and stuff like that, but my dad's can access our home's generator and internal programming since he and my mom are the primary licensees.

"You a brainie, huh? That was bop," the boy said. I helped him up and slipped his comm device back on his wrist.

"Brainie" refers to the one type of artificial organ that doesn't exist, also because of the referendum. People just couldn't handle the idea of printing someone's brain out; I think it had to do with identity or consciousness, something like that. I only skimmed the articles and my dad hasn't explained that one yet. So, now we just use it to describe people whose intelligence is boomer high.

"Want me to page a first-aid drone?" I offered.

"Drones suck. Let's find the ice cream machine."

I walked after him, sensing this wasn't his first time being targeted and that he had some kind of recovery practice he followed. We selected our ingredients from the digital menu. I ordered fresh mint and Mateo got the same thing but added every possible topping. The screen cleared so we could see the machine inside churn the cream and sugar with mint and then package the food. After the final product was dropped through the slot, he held the cold packet to his forehead and sighed with relief.

"Can I help you home?" I offered.

"No, thanks, I have to get to my beach cleanup."

We tapped our wrists to swap contact info and I spent the rest of the afternoon doing homework and tracking him under the #lifeisbeautifulgov or #organgratitude social networks as he worked, piling trash into strangely elegant piles before they were scooped up. Volunteer faces were blurred to protect people's privacy and keep them safe, but I could make out Mateo's ears, and I think, the bruise on his forehead. I could also see the protestors kept at a distance behind metal fences, carrying signs with pictures of bloody robots beneath headlines that said, "God doesn't speak C++" or "Machine life is an abomination."

8

Chapter 2

My earliest memory is of discovering the vertical scar down my chest. Here is how I remember it:

Childhood Memory

Detailed Mental Review While I'm Supposed to be Doing Homework

I am almost three. House is set to Bath—the water just as hot as I like it, a warmer bathroom temperature, and my favorite towel with bunny ears being fluffed up in the dryer. My mom is scrubbing my back, a job she insists on doing herself because, again, my parents are kind of old-fashioned. Also, my mom's a nursing assistant to a Medical AI, which means that she goes into people's homes to carry out the orders it gives, like putting in IVs or holding patient's hands and asking how they are, things like that. She believes in skin-to-skin contact, even if it means struggling with a wet and soapy toddler and even if there's a robot programmed to be ready and willing to serve.

9

It is a faint scar, shiny and more slippery than the rest of my skin. I tuck my chin to see the length of it and curiously touch the faded pink line with my finger.

"Mama, what this?"

"That's the scar from your surgery, Obie," she answers. Her lips are pink. Her straight, brown hair covers her shoulders.

"What sugewey?" I ask.

"Surgery is when the doctor and her robot fix some tidbits inside your body."

"What fix?"

"Just your heart needed help, that's all," she says. "Now it's fixed and strong. And soon your chest will smell nice from the cream I rub in."

I continue to trace the line on my breastbone, thinking and piecing a few things together.

"Why Mama rub cream?"

"To help fix the scar, Obie."

"But heart fixed."

"Yes. You are strong and safe and healthy. You are great as you are," she reassures me.

"So why Mama rub cream?"

My mom's hands pause as she washes my hair. She gently squeezes my ear lobes and then massages my neck. "We are going to stop using that cream now. There is nothing to fix. Nothing to rub in or out."

I still have a scar today (I told you we were old-fashioned). I could get rid of it in a week, but something won't let me. Sometimes I wonder what would happen if I were to walk up to those Humanists with their bloody signs and open my shirt to expose the mark. I imagine myself with outstanding posture, my chin up, my eyes bold. Then I picture their shocked expressions changing to hatred as they start chasing me, throwing stones at my head. Then I decide to snap out of my fantasy.

I guess you're wondering why I know so much about referendums while everyone else my age is zoning out. Take, for example, my best friend before Mateo. Her name was Stella, and since the fifth grade I've only seen her outside of school in virtual spaces. She barely even talks to me in there. Most kids these days are just like her.

Well, my dad is a policy wonk, working for America along with two bots that are focused on production and exports. I think that in a previous life he was a robed philosopher teaching kids on top of a mountain because he's always clasping his hands behind his back and looking up with a sigh. When my mom and I have stopped giggling, he usually starts lecturing. I like to make up quotes just to get him started so we can get the whole thing over with fast. Like the other day House was set to dinner when Dad stood, gave his big sigh and walked over to the window, gazing out at all the other sky rises. I was too hungry to wait for him to begin, so I said, "George Washington once said, 'Gosh, I hate this hat. Triangular hats make for triangular hair, heads, and therefore ideas.'"

My mom was looking down at her console, but I could see her shoulders start shaking with laughter. She's one of the few people who like my sense of humor.

"Ba," House said. "You are mocking Father."

Ba is what House calls me because that's what I used to say when I started mimicking my parents giving House commands. "Ba turn off movie. Ba give Korean ice cream." I guess you could say that Ba was the first voice command I gave that wasn't crying. No one knew what it meant, not even House, but I think it meant, "I'm here too so listen up."

Anyway, Dad ignored me. "Mankind used to suffer from a high prevalence of obesity," he began. I'd heard this one before, so I knew he'd call on me. Also, I was the only young person there. "Obie, what was obesity?"

"Obesity was extreme overweight," I dutifully answered.

"And what caused obesity?" he probed, his light blue eyes looking outside.

"More energy being saved than spent."

"Exactly," he confirmed, turning to face me. "But that's not all." He brushed his sandy brown hair off his forehead.

I perked up. Usually this went right into a lecture on getting some exercise out of basic tasks, like when we set House to rest and cooked our own food.

"Obesity also came from economic inefficiency," he continued.

"How's that?" I asked.

"You tell me," he countered.

"Uh," I tried to break it down in my head. "Can I look something up?"

"You can have one encyclopedia use."

"House, was exercise ever completely unreachable for people?" I asked.

"Ba," House answered, "exercise was generally available via outdoor activity, including in public spaces such as parks, or indoor activity such as jumping rope and gymnasium use. However, working conditions could make exercise difficult for many to complete regularly, as could physical injuries. Genetic predispositions to energy conservation also caused various exercises to be less impactful for some."

"Dad," I asked. "Did you tell House I was older again?" House is usually calibrated to make answers understandable to a teenager.

"Challenge yourself, Obie," Dad replied.

"Fine," I said. "I think that a market surplus of food caused a lot of obesity. Like those shelves full of ready-made meals and potato chips in big bags I've seen photos of."

"What about costs, Obie?" Dad was never satisfied with a one-part answer.

"Um, food must have been cheap. Or—bad food must have been cheap. Maybe there were government subsidies or something."

"Or something?" He hated it when I said "something."

"Well, maybe people also didn't know what was bad for them. Maybe they didn't read the labels on food we used to have before there was AI to tell us what to buy or just do the shopping for us," I added.

"Very thought-provoking arguments, Obie. In fact, today food prices are calibrated to reflect the societal cost of obesity.

13

It went to a referendum called VEG OUT about fifty years ago, and it passed. This is why fresh vegetables are so affordable."

Policies always go to a vote when AI detects a conflict between human feeling and all other economic variables. My dad says this is more to subdue a revolution than because the AI values our opinions; if the AI senses that people have more resistance to artificially generated ideas than a society can handle without imploding, it asks us to decide for ourselves. My dad calls it the, "You don't like it, you deal with it," of policy making.

"Is that why you named me Obie? To remind me people used to be obese, and that was unhealthy?" I looked down at my knobby knees. They were sticking out more than usual. *Was that supposed to be good now?*

"No." My mom looked up from the news digest she was reading on her console and put her hand on mine. "Obie means 'servant of God.' We named you Obie so our daughter would never be a servant of technology and would keep her own wisdom and goodness in her beautiful heart."

We are not particularly religious, and I was surprised to hear that. So, I learned a few things that day.

The next afternoon after school I tagged along with my mom on a house call to Mrs. Stein. She's 120 years old and can remember things like when America was divided into 50 states. I've been coming along since I was five years old. I like to look out her windows—they have actual curtains on them—and I get to sit on her dark wooden chairs with pink cushions. When I was younger, I would race my toy horses on the

14

pathways marked by the pattern on her Persian rug, which looks like it's as old as her.

My mom really likes Mrs. Stein because she used to be a trauma nurse and has all sorts of stories from the days when nursing was harder and bloodier. Mrs. Stein says that she "liked the rush," an old-fashioned saying that always cracks Mom and I up because she says it with a really innocent expression while serving us tea with rugelach cookies.

On our visits, Mom administers a gene therapy infusion to stabilize the allelic repetition that gave Mrs. Stein the pre-mutation for a disease called Fragile X Syndrome. The way my mom explains it, Mrs. Stein doesn't have a full-fledged genetic sickness, but there is enough going on in the area of her DNA that would have caused the disease to trigger a few other symptoms. In her case, it's enough to make her face twitch involuntarily. Nowadays this won't happen in babies born with this kind of thing, but Mrs. Stein has the older therapy in her system and sometimes it comes undone, in which case Mom gives her a tune up.

"Obie, honey, I can't believe how tall you are! How did you grow so fast?" Mrs. Stein asked me.

"I don't know. Can we ask your House?"

"My house is set to shut up, darling. A good house is seen and not heard," Mrs. Stein said.

"Obie has been feeling self-conscious about her knees," my mom said as she hooked up the equipment under the watchful gaze of her AI.

"Mom."

"What's wrong with your knees, dearie?" Mrs. Stein asked. She was the only person I'd ever let call me "dearie." It made me feel warm when she said it, but that was because she was special.

"Nothing, they're just really knobby. Like, I could hang my hat on them." It's true. After my dad's lecture I realized that my legs look like the bars of the speed rail.

"Women once had surgery to get your slender physique, Obie," Mrs. Stein said. "They had their fat cells sucked out or frozen off."

I've heard this before, but I find it hard to believe, even when I peek at fashion images from a hundred years ago. All the celebrities these days are having synthetic fat—it looks just like foam—stuffed into their bodies to look more overweight and voluptuous. They keep sharing images where they're lying in repose, like a woman in a Renaissance painting with dimpled thighs. My dad says people want to look a bit overweight because high fashion is defined by what's out-of-reach for most and fatty food is now priced sky high because of the obesity thing.

"My daughter had your physique," Mrs. Stein said.

Mom and I both paused—me with rugelach in my hand before my open mouth, and her with her equipment.

"You've never mentioned a daughter," Mom said.

"Ah, some memories best lay buried. I lost her when she was young."

Stories of people who die young usually get played on late-night TV or stuck in the "Beloved Classics" category near military stories with in-person battles and tons of blood.

I kept quiet because I didn't know what to say and my dad always said it is better to wait until you do.

"We are so sad to hear that," Mom said, turning her entire body to face Mrs. Stein.

"It was an undiagnosed heart defect. She collapsed during a physical education class at school one day and that was it." Mrs. Stein looked at me thoughtfully. "Obie, all life is a miracle, whether it is chubby or knobby."

I sat there silently and nodded. Later my mom would compliment me for knowing when to keep quiet because sometimes silence is the best response; but the truth is that I really had no idea what to say. *A heart defect? Was it like mine? Could Mrs. Stein possibly know my secret?* I wondered.

My mom put her hand on Ms. Stein's hand and said, "Yes, I know what you mean about miracles. It's why I became a nurse." She stepped out to get equipment from our vehicle. I wish she'd stayed because I was frozen, feeling nervous and then guilty, and I couldn't look at Mrs. Stein right then. I know it seems selfish, but I felt sorry for myself in a twisted way. I mean, while other teens at school are obsessed with keeping their clothes fashionable, or even making sure their avatars' wardrobes are on trend, I only think about how much I hate how people like me are called Mooches. Or how I can't defend myself without outing myself. I never think about miracles. I ponder over how I'm so tired of being different, hidden, and hated for getting a transplant. Even when my dad brought up the obesity thing and I felt bad about my knees, I realized I wasn't thinking about my closeted heart and that was a relief for a few minutes.

I think the seed of all of my emotions was planted in my mind in the bathtub when I was three, touching the scar on my chest, and then those feelings sprouted into a small plant when I saw that drone attack Mateo. Also, if I ever get a break, I'll happen to walk by a Humanist protest or their ads against people like me. Sometimes their digital posters will show the supposed insides of artificial transplant recipients. Our faces are always intact but frozen, our eyes expressionless, and our abdomens cut open to reveal mechanical intestines dripping with oil. Usually there's a caption like, "You can't manufacture a soul" or "Real eyes see abomination."

It's as if I were born wrong somehow and now exist in a way that people will never see, not even if they do an autopsy when I die. My life is buried inside me, if that makes any sense.

I know I'm being lamezy for being so pissed at my situation when I could be dead, like Mrs. Stein's daughter. I should be grateful for being alive, but it's hard to be that way all the time. I suppose that for Mateo it's different because he must have some memory of partial blindness so he can appreciate his new cornea even if it means being able to see the trash he cleans up more clearly. I just wish death wasn't my comparison, that's all, and that I couldn't relate to stories of dead girls with heart defects.

Mrs. Stein rolled her wheelchair close to me and then changed it to standing support as she looked out the window at kids playing baseball in the parklet. A little boy hit the ball directly toward our window and I flinched even as the hologram evaporated before it hit the pane. "The problem with people today," Mrs. Stein continued, "is that they take life for granted. They assume they'll reach one hundred and twenty and all the bumps along the way will be fixed for them."

"I don't assume that," I said. I sounded like I was whimpering. A few strands of my light brown hair rose to stick to the curtains because of the static cling.

"I didn't mean to sound so harsh, dearie," Mrs. Stein said. "I learned this the hard way—the main way to realize life is a miracle is to experience the loss of one, an event I hope you never know. And one day I looked at these other kids and realized that I had to content myself with the continuation of humanity instead of my own child. I have done that as a nurse and I'm grateful for the opportunity, because otherwise I'd be unable to get through the days."

I thought that moment would be a good one to use humor to lighten a mood. Then I remembered that I tell bad jokes.

"I see all children as beautiful miracles because life is a miracle that they hold. It's a fact you understand when you hold a baby and smell their tiny head," she continued. And then Mrs. Stein looked right at me, her milky but bright blue eyes examining me closely. "And I don't care how that life came to be or what it is inside of. It's life that's the miracle, not the container."

I felt myself break out in goose bumps at her words. "What was your daughter's name?" I asked to change the topic a little.

"Nava," she answered. "In Hebrew it means beautiful."

19

Chapter 3

"Total coincidence," Mateo said. "No way Mrs. Stein could have known about your heart. Your mom would have had to have told her, and she wouldn't. She didn't even know about Nava until now. It wouldn't have even come up." We were sitting on the roof deck of my building and had the whole thing to ourselves. Above us, fumes from the city touched the biodome and fizzled as they were absorbed for reuse. And thirteen stories down on the street, Humanists were protesting loudly. My chat with Mateo was interrupted by the annoying banging of drums and snippets of angry chanting. *Bang bang . . . (muffled) . . . God's code . . . (muffled) . . . DNA not . . . (muffled) . . . bang!*

"What a great soundtrack for this conversation," Mateo said. "I think they've figured out how to angle their speakers to bypass the noise pollution filter."

"Yeah," I said. "If they stand almost right below them, their sound waves are pretty much uninterrupted." The pattern of *bang, yell, cheer* was still firing off in the distance.

"Their chanting sounds like gunfire. How come these people hate us so much?"

"Because it makes them feel good. Hatred needs to feel smug with itself." He flicked a grasshopper-flour cookie into his mouth. He had built a spiraled pyramid of them on his palm. It was actually very pretty.

"I couldn't eat those unless I were blind and didn't know what they were," I said.

"That's because you've seen actual grasshoppers, because your parents are hippie granola people."

"That's true," I admitted. Mateo's parents are like many—very happy to set their house to automatic when it comes to food delivery and prep and to know nothing about what comes next. I was snacking on chips my dad had made using beans he grew in clear planter boxes on our balcony. They crumbled before they entered my mouth. A pigeon perched nearby and watched me with great interest.

"Don't look at me," I said to the bird, pointing at Mateo. "That guy is actually eating bugs."

"Don't make the birdie hate me too," Mateo said. "Creatures who don't fight over morals always fight over food."

"You think that's mostly what people fight over? Why?" I asked, picking up one of his cookies and examining it closely. It felt dense and heavy like a stone.

"Interesting question, Obie," Mateo put his cookies down, then stood and clasped his hands behind his back in clear imitation of my father. I snorted with laughter. "I say that, perhaps, when bellies are full, people search for other ways to feel even better."

"So, it's a hierarchy of needs," I probed, ignoring his innuendo and borrowing from the latest psychology text we'd just been tested on in school. It was an old theory. Next, we were going to learn about the idea that no one knew what they needed until they saw someone else with it. I think it grew out of studies on social media and depression.

"Yes, and only when people are not hungry can their minds turn to other topics, including their need to feel good about themselves as people, which they get by hating us."

"So, basically you're saying that if all the Humanists were hungry, they'd become totally preoccupied and leave us alone."

Mateo nodded and gave me his extra-twinkle-in-his-blue-eye look. I've only seen that look a few other times, usually when some good-looking guy passes us on the street and both our heads turn. Then he bowed, sat back down, and ate another grasshopper cookie.

"Or," I continued, holding a cookie in my hand, "we could flip that around. If Humanists were busy eating in order to avoid hunger, then they'd leave us alone." I looked down at the protestors and picked up a grasshopper cookie. "I wonder if they are in the mood for dessert."

"Obie, I may only understand half of what you're thinking, but be careful."

"Relax, *amigo*," I said. "I am undetectable."

"What are you talking about?" Mateo asked. "You know there are security cameras above us."

"Yeah, but I also know that in a few minutes they'll be covered in fog, just for a short time."

"Eh?"

"It has to do with the air conditioning and pollution filters. Before a cleaning cycle, the air filter above us makes some ice. Then the chemicals dancing around the pollution filters hit them, and we end up with a really quick but thick and icy fog, right in front of the security cameras."

"How do you know all this crapola?" he asked.

"House told me."

"But Houses aren't supposed to help crime."

"Well, House didn't mention the security camera part...I may have indirectly investigated why I didn't get into trouble when I spilled ten bottles of glitter up here on the roof deck when I was seven," I admitted.

"You mean you weren't caught on camera?"

"No, I happened to have the accident at the right time, so the lens was blocked by fog. I didn't even clean up the glitter and no one knew it was me."

"That's bop. Also, it explains why whenever we leave here, I sparkle more than usual."

I was going to laugh, then heard the ambient *bang, go, bang, hell, bang, you, whistle, cheer*. I felt my cheeks flush. *Enough already*, I thought.

"Anyway, if people who think about food don't think about hatred, I think I should probably remind them about dessert." I aimed and then threw two handfuls of cookies as far upwards as I could, right towards the air duct above us in the biodome. The cookies spun in the circle of the current and were then shot sideways and outwards, past the border of our building. As they fell down, Mateo and I rushed to the clear fence at the side and looked at the street. We couldn't see the cookies, but the regular chant of the protest suddenly changed from well-organized, distinct words to a mess of cries. So, I took another handful of grasshopper cookies and tossed them too. Mateo, with a look of pure glee, emptied the rest of the box. And then, the best, most unplanned thing happened. Our friendly pigeon swept past our heads and flew down to the street to pick up the mess. What could be better than grasshopper cookies? He was joined by about twenty of his pigeon friends, zooming around the Humanists heads, making them scream. Mateo and I looked at each other, then down, then at each other, and then started laughing so hard we had to wipe our eyes. We ran to the elevator and took it to the ground level for an up-close view, which was even better than I'd expected. Even more birds had joined the party and Humanists were batting at the air with their posters, most of which were getting covered with bird poop and feathers. I decided that the grand prize, even if I'm not sure for what, had to go to one plump woman with unnaturally large thighs and arms that were probably pumped with synthetic fat. She was standing tall, trying to look fierce, with a digitized sign bearing alternating messages that the smeared bird droppings blocked. So, what was probably supposed to be, "God owns the copyright to my DNA!" became an interesting statement: "copyright my [poop]!" "The road to Hell is paved with good intentions and bad code" was also adorned with bird droppings and feathers, making it read: "The road to Hell is paved with [poop] and [feathers]." I thought it looked pretty accurate right then.

"Obie, I don't think you fed those guys anything," Mateo said, giggling and putting his hands on his knees so he could breathe.

"That's okay, maybe they'll think it was a sign from God."

We hugged and he walked off to catch the rail to his volunteer work. I stood there for a few more minutes, taking in the chaos. It was the first time I'd ever looked at Humanists with a feeling other than fear and anger.

"Obie?"

I turned around. It was Stella, my friend from school who had ditched me years before. She looked gorgeous as usual; her straight blond hair reached past her shoulders and her pants accentuated her natural curves.

"Hi, Stella, what are you doing all the way out here?" I could have added, "And why are you talking to me?" because she always ignores me, even though we visit the same virtual game rooms.

"My mom and I are doing some shopping," she answered quickly.

"That's bop. I hope you brought a good umbrella," I said. She stared at me, looking confused. I pointed to the birds right as one relieved himself on the sidewalk.

"Oh, right," she said. I felt myself blush. My jokes are always lamezy. "Are you hanging out with Mateo?" she asked.

"No, he just left."

"Hopefully not to clean this?" Stella asked, smiling widely and gesturing at the mess.

I shook my head no.

"It would be a nice day for the beach," she said, "if all the birds are here."

"I think that may be where he's headed," I said, wondering why she was asking me about Mateo.

"Scraper in hand, just in case?" Stella made a scrubbing motion, smiling widely. I wished she'd let go of the bird thing. The conversation felt really forced and awkward enough.

"I think the scrapers are provided for them."

"Gotcha. Well, it was nice bumping into you." Stella kept up her overly large smile.

"Have fun shopping with your mom."

"Huh? Oh, yes, thanks."

I turned and nearly walked into a woman who was swearing and trying to wash her crap-covered hair off in a public fountain. She looked up at me and yelled, "WHAT ARE YOU LOOKING AT?"

I looked at her shirt. It had a diagram of a monster with machine parts inside his body painted on the front. The heart was made up of a bunch of cogs. I raised my finger and pointed to it, feeling the words move up my throat and slide down my tongue. I wanted to tell her that picture was me but also wasn't me, that on the inside I was just human. I would never treat others as badly as she did, so I was a better human than her. I must have been drunk on the power I felt from the pigeon fiasco because I'd never wanted to come out more, but as I opened my mouth, she turned her body and stood, leaning over me. "What's the matter, honey?" she snarled, her hot breath smothering my face. "The devil got your tongue? He'll sort you out soon enough."

My blood cooled fast. I turned around and ran home.

Childhood Memory

Detailed Mental Review While Lying on My Bed After Bumping into Stella

Stella and I are around nine years old. We are partners in an augmented reality scavenger hunt at school. We have decided to split up to cover more ground while hunting for tokens. Whoever gets the most tokens wins a trophy—a golden apple, one per person. We both really want to win. We're talking to each other using our headsets as she scavenges the school building and I search the field. We're down to the last clue and token: "Don't rush, this must be mounted just right." The subject is American landmarks.

I'm running and panting. We can see how the other teams are doing in a rectangular, vertical grid displayed in our goggle view; most are placed way lower than us but there's one other team shown as a flashing yellow light near the top and right next to us. They must also be down to the last token, and we don't want to come in second place.

I scan the field. The scavenger hunt organizers have placed fragmented images across our view plate. When I look around, the images lay on top of the real world. If they fit into the real world and form a complete picture, like puzzle pieces into the larger image, we'll see the answer to the puzzle and get a token. When the images fit it's like watching a mirage become real. The ones on my display now are of tiny, fluffy

27

white pieces. I look up at the clouds and try to align them, but it doesn't click. "Don't rush"—*What did that mean? Was it part of the clue?*

"Obie," Stella says, "I've searched everywhere but the art studios and the cafeteria."

This must be mounted; I recall from the clue.

"Go to the art studios," I tell her. "Look for mounted photos."

She shares her view with me as she enters the first classroom. There are printed black-and-white photos lying around everywhere. I don't know how we're supposed to look through them all.

"I don't know what to do," Stella says.

"Look for anything mounted," I tell her. She scans the room and we see an empty wooden frame hanging against the wall.

"Now what?" she asks me. In my goggle view, I see the flashing yellow light of our competitors. The pace seems to intensify. I want the trophy.

Mounted just right, I think. The frame is crooked. "Stella, straighten the frame. Lift up the right corner a bit." She shifts the edge and I see it one moment before she does. There's a tiny photo that was hidden by the frame. It looks like the outline of faces. "Stella!" I hiss.

"I see it!" she squeals. She backs up and looks at the photo intently. The white fragments we've been given on our view panes align perfectly with the photograph, blending into the parts on the page seamlessly. Suddenly we're looking at the image of Mount Rushmore.

YOU WIN flashes across both our screens. We each start shrieking, jumping, and clapping—her in the art studio, me in the field.

At the awards ceremony we embrace in front of the entire class. Holding the trophy in my hands feels even better than I thought it would. Stella and I smile for a photo and are interviewed for the school newspaper. I wake up early the next morning to see the article as soon as it goes live. The photo is of Stella looking down at her golden apple. The sunlight reflects off the surface and illuminates her green eyes and blonde hair. I must be standing in the shadows somewhere, physically and otherwise, because the caption says "Young winner Stella admires her prize!" and you have to read well into the article to find my name.

I wonder where I put that dang apple. I think I threw it away.

Chapter 4

That afternoon Mom and I were planning to visit Mrs. Stein for her cataract surgery. I'd never seen a procedure before and Mrs. Stein told my mom she'd be happy for me to observe in person. We arrived at her house just as the robot and sterile kiosk were being delivered. I sat on the floor, trying to see if I could circle my kneecaps with my thumb and index fingers, while my mom set everything up. I wanted to ask Mrs. Stein about hatred, if she thought it needed to feel smug with itself like Mateo believed, but I wasn't sure how to bring it up.

"Obie, I'd like to introduce you to Dr. Kerwin," Mom said, gesturing towards the console. I walked over and saw a woman wearing large goggles. Behind her, I could see that it was snowing outside her window.

"Nice to meet you," she said, waving at me with her gloved hand. "I love working with your mom!"

"Thanks for letting me observe today."

"Nicola," my mom said, "Robot is up and I'm almost done blocking the kiosk."

"Want to try out the robot while your mom gets everything ready?" the surgeon asked me.

"Seriously? Yeah!" That was really exciting; I loved robots but so far had only used one to clean our house during chores.

"It's always good to mentor the next generation of clinicians," Mrs. Stein chimed in, smiling.

"Okay, there are a pair of student goggles and gloves in Robot's cubby hole," Dr. Kerwin said. I opened a small door on the side of the machine and pulled them out. "Put the goggles on first, then the gloves." I followed her instruction, flinching a bit as these tools shrank to fit around my head and fingers. I was gazing at a blue electronic screen. "Okay," she continued. "I'm going to activate education mode." Her voice was now piped directly into my ear. There was a tiny beep, then the video changed from the blue screen to the image of an eyeball, its lids pulled back and held out of the way. I gasped, not because of that, but more because I had the sensation that I was no longer fully in charge of my hands, although they were still attached to my body. "You'll get used to it," Dr. Kerwin said.

"To what?" I heard Mrs. Stein ask in the background.

"I think the term is 'marionette puppet,'" the doctor answered.

I didn't know what those puppets were. All I could think of was having my hands guided by my VR piano instructor before my dad turned it off and placed his own hands over mine. Now my lack of full control brought on a feeling that mixed parental reassurance with fear. It was like when I was learning to use my hover sneakers and they braked when I came too close to the curb, a second before my parents, my flesh-and-blood guardians, grabbed my hands and pulled me back.

"Pick up the scalpel," Dr. Kerwin said.

"But Mom is setting up the tray, and everything has been sterilized."

"Look up and to the right."

I obeyed and saw a virtual surgical tray that enlarged and became front-and-center in my view when I focused on it. CATARACT SURGERY was emblazoned above it. STUDENT MODE. Each tool had labels floating above it. I saw a white object further up and right that expanded when I stared right at it. It was a checklist. A number of items had already been marked off, like "Emergency kit status" and "Confirm patient ID."

"I gave you a head start," the doctor said. "Your patient is anesthetized and I've checked the corneal status. I've also mapped the eye surface, so we know the location of the lens. Let's practice creating a conjunctival incision."

"A what?" I'd started sweating. The eyeball stared at me. I think the expression was saying, *Don't mess me up or I'll haunt you.*

"It's the cut we'll use to extract the cloudy cataract and put in a new, artificial one."

I tried not to flinch at the word "artificial." It actually was the correct use of the word. My mom had told me Mrs. Stein would get one made from synthetic parts.

"Direct Robot to pick up the crescent knife," Dr. Kerwin instructed. I looked at the surgical tray, and without reading the label, moved my hand toward a tool that was long and pointy. My hand froze—or maybe I should say it was frozen—mid-air. A low beep sounded. "That tool is the ultrasound instrument," she said. "Look for a cutting tool." As the surgeon spoke, a pen-like tool started glowing and my gloved hand was guided towards it. When I picked it up, it vibrated briefly and then I felt its weight in my hand. I shifted my gaze outside the goggles and saw that Robot was holding the instrument in real life. I wondered who was controlling who.

"Now, Obie, I can see that you're a bit nervous. Are you alright making an incision? I know it looks real. You can say no."

I thought back to the Humanist protest that morning and how disgusted the protesters were with transplant recipients. Would they turn against people like Mrs. Stein for wanting to see, even if it meant putting synthetic material in their eye? Then I thought about Mrs. Stein's point that life is a miracle, no matter its container, and I decided that I didn't want to be afraid of the medical field, even though I was pretty scared right now.

"I'm ready to see what's inside," I said. For some reason I had a pang where I missed Mateo a lot, even though we'd just spent the morning together.

"Okay, Obie." The middle of the colorful part of the eye lit up. "Bring the knife to the outside border of the cornea, holding it so that the blade lays flat." I did so. Robot moved my hand so the blade lay even closer to the virtual eye, so I could feel its bounciness pressing back against my tool. "Now we're going to make the incision. Take a deep breath and press gently forward and down." So, I did, trying not to shriek as the tiny blade went into the squishy virtual eyeball. Robot stopped me from pushing further and then I drew my hand back. "Very good, Obie!" Dr. Kerwin said. "Now put down the blade and pick up the ultrasound tool you tried to get earlier." If my hand was shaking, Robot didn't let it show. *Good machine.* "Insert the tool into the incision you just made," she continued.

"Eh? I've got to go back in there?" I asked.

"Yep. If you don't want to cut this patient for nothing."

Gingerly, I pressed the tool into the area where I'd just cut. It was like playing with jelly. I tried to not notice the eye staring at me blindly. The gismo I was holding slid back in.

"Now turn it on," she said. Robot and I pressed a button and light streamed out of the instrument. My view zoomed in to the center of the eye where the lens broke apart like a gelatinous earthquake. I truly hoped my knobby knees could hold me up. "You are breaking up the lens so we can get it out of there. Good. Now suction it all up." Robot and I pressed another button, and all the lens-gelatin stuff was sucked into our tool. "Excellent work, Obie. Now take out the ultrasound probe." We slid it gently out. I sort of ignored the way the eye jiggled a bit. "Last step, Obie. Use the tweezers-like tool to insert the intraocular lens. I'll help you here." The tool appeared magically in my hand with a clear and small circular lens in its grasp. Robot and I moved our hand back into the incision we'd created and shoved the synthetic cornea into place as gently as possible. It unfolded to fit the space and

Call Me Obie

made me think of the elbow patches on my dad's sweaters. As we took our tool out of the eye one last time, Dr. Kerwin said, "Good job, Obie! You can take the gloves and goggles off now."

Back in the room, my mom was staring at me and smiling a little. "Nice work, daughter-of-mine," she said. Mrs. Stein looked a bit worried, though.

"Isn't my procedure going to be done with lasers?" she asked, looking over at Dr. Kerwin on the console.

"Yes, but manual work is the best way to learn," she answered.

"You mean I didn't have to do it that way?!" I exclaimed, louder than I meant to.

"Hey, you want to learn or what?" The surgeon and everyone else laughed. I tried to join in, but my head felt fuzzy and I was noticing the way my hands were strangely tired and heavy having to move on their own.

Mrs. Stein's procedure took about fifteen minutes, most of which I didn't really notice because I was thinking too much about my own experience.

"I'm so proud of you, Obie," my mom said, wrapping her arm around my shoulders as we waited for our vehicle. "Or, as you would say, 'that was bop.' And next thing I know, you'll be a brain surgeon."

"Could I?"

"Why not? You're so talented," she said.

"I mean, could that robot also do brain surgery?"

35

"If it had the right tools available, it would just need to connect to the right protocols and surgeon," she told me.

"Wow." I was so excited to tell Mateo. Maybe one day I'd be an eye surgeon and just fix his blue eye already and that was it, no more volunteering for him to do. I was going to ask my mom more, but just then our comms vibrated with an emergency communication: MASS CASUALTY EVENT. STAY HOME OR INDOORS. INFORMATION SECURITY ASSESSMENT UNDERWAY. EXPECTED SYSTEMWIDE DISRUPTION TO LAST ONE HOUR.

"What?"

My mom's arm tightened around my shoulder as she looked up. Our vehicle landed in front of us, and she waved her comm in front of the carriage door frantically, but it wouldn't open. She tapped her palm against the window but of course that didn't do anything.

"What's going on?" I asked.

"I don't know." She looked around. People everywhere seemed just as confused. They were tapping their comms as if that would fix them, then looking around suspiciously while taking a few steps in one direction, changing course, and coming back to where they were. Around and above us, vehicles were slowing to a stop and then lowering to park on the street. Within one minute the roads were clogged, and after letting their passengers out, a few parked stacked on top of others.

People left their office buildings and joined the rest of the muddled crowd that was beginning to grow. Outside of their murmur, the world felt suddenly quiet, like when the noise of people talking at a party spontaneously drops so you only hear one or two voices. I think I must have gotten used to the low hum of our artificial environment, and when it was gone, its absence was almost vulgar.

We got another message: EMERGENCY COMM MODE ENABLED.

"What's emergency comm mode? What is going on?" I put my hands on my stomach and tried to breathe in deeply but couldn't.

"It means we can call each other but that's about it," she said. "I'm going to call your dad." She pulled an earpiece out of her bag. I hadn't seen one of those in years; I always used the invisible sound cone on mine. For a moment I was grateful for my old-fashioned parents. While she talked to my dad, I wandered back up the steps to Mrs. Stein's retirement community and peered through the glass doors, wondering if we should just go back inside and have some rugelach. My mom walked up behind me. "Obie," she said, sounding strained, "let's walk home."

"What happened?"

"The details are still coming in, but your dad says it's safe to walk home...Everything is fine."

I've always known when my mom is lying, mostly because she's bad at it—her eyebrows furrow and she nods her head—but also because she does it so rarely that it's easy to identify. I was sure it was safe to walk home if she said so, but also sure that nothing was fine, that whatever had happened was even worse than I could imagine.

It took us forty-five minutes to get back when normally I think it would have taken twenty. The sidewalks overflowed with people and the traffic lights changed on timers instead of detecting and responding to our movement and volume. I didn't understand why one event would cause multiple systems to be shut off. Once, we'd had an upgrade of the speed rail information system after it didn't accurately report corrosion of some of the train parts, but that didn't call for everything else to be rebooted.

We all started out as confused individuals and became a confused mass, like a lump of insects climbing over each other while buzzing in sync. A few people clustered around speed rail stations, sitting on the pavement, and resigning themselves to waiting. Behind me, one woman was pointing extravagantly down the street and saying to the other, "You go about four blocks that way, and then I think you turn left in front of that brown building at the corner of D Street. I'm almost certain." I realized why my dad was always telling me to use my brain. I knew the way home easily.

I spotted another knot of people wearing VR goggles and gazing into space. When we walked closer, I heard one of them saying, "Spin isn't working either, everything is totally down."

"I was in the middle of the nicest beach," complained one of them.

"We could have asked them to navigate us," said another.

I realized they were all using the EmpathSpin app, and I felt pretty jealous. The app lets you see through another person's eyes. You could also make yourself available and people would just "enter" your space and get to see your world from your point of view. If you were really brave, you could set yourself up for random matches instead of picking and choosing based on profiles. My parents had blocked from me from it and I felt like I was really missing out.

My mom took my hand and pulled me forward, snapping me back to the present. One woman who was staring at her non-functional comm and tapping it furiously, walked into my mom, looked up startled, and then burst into tears. I've seen people like that before, the ones who won't ever let go, who wear theirs in the shower and in bed at night. When the woman started crying, my mom put her hands on the woman's arms and craned her neck down to force eye contact. "It will be okay; breathe. You will be fine." The woman tried to inhale but it sounded jagged. "Try again; you are okay." The woman inhaled deeply. "Now let it out slowly. You are okay." The woman obeyed and I saw her shoulders, which were bunched around her neck, relax a bit. She nodded and walked away. "Some people are more addicted to the hand motions and the electronic interaction than to the communication itself," my mom explained to me. Sometimes I think she has superpowers.

We arrived at our building covered in sweat. As I started up the front steps, my mom put her hand on my shoulder and said, "You know, if you weighed a lot more, that would have been much harder on your body." *Nice try*, I thought, but I still found myself standing a little straighter as I opened the small slide covering the retinal scanner entry key. Nothing happened. As I remembered we were in emergency mode, my dad opened the door for us.

"Hello, ladies," he said with a forced smile.

"What is going on?!" I asked when we were inside. "House, two ice waters please!" Nothing happened. I waved my hand in front of the refrigerator. Silence. I'd never realized how accustomed I was to House greeting me when I got home, which I guess it had been doing since I was in kindergarten. I turned to face my parents, feeling fear override the determination I'd felt in getting home. My mom looked at my dad. She had the brow furrow again. Was she debating lying to me?

"Obie," my dad said, putting his arm around my shoulders and guiding me to the couch. The footrest didn't automatically open and rise. I plopped down and tucked my legs underneath me. "There was a shooting today."

"A what?"

"A shooting. Many police officers' guns opened fire on a crowd."

"Why would they do that?"

"They didn't. They were armed with guns that could only be used with a retinal scan for identity verification in addition to a few other nearly instantaneous factors, like co-location of the gun and the person allowed to use it. Their guns were hacked with a bug that somehow copied their retinal scans and then convinced Security AI they were authentic. It was a weakness in the manufacturer's information system."

"You mean their own guns were used without their permission, in their own hands?"

"Yes."

I felt this knee-jerk need to ask House how many times anything like this had happened. And why things like this happened. And how it could still happen. My mom crouched in front of me and put her hand on mine.

"Obie, there's more. The police were guarding a group of volunteers at a clean-up."

"What kind of volunteers?"

"Transplant recipients."

My heart fell into my stomach.

"Obie, breathe," my mom said. My dad started rubbing my back. I tried to inhale but it got stuck between my shoulder blades. My mom gently unfolded my legs and brought my head down to my knees. "Breathe." She pressed her fingers against the top of my scalp, the sides of my face, my sides, and my wrists. As she repeated this, I felt the edge of calm wash towards me like a wave before it was sucked away again by fear and anger. I needed to know a piece of information, but I could not get the words out. I stammered and choked instead.

"Mateo was injured but he's alive, and in the hospital," my dad said.

The waves of emotion reached me and then overcame me. I started to cry and my parents let me. If House had been working, I could have told you for how long.

"Can I see him?" I finally said.

"I can take you to the hospital once the transport system is back up," my mom said.

Then we all heard this dinging sound and turned our heads upward, which is where we always look at House although House is all around us.

"Security upgrade complete. Multi-factor authentication enabled. Security report available." House sounded more robotic than I'd ever heard.

"House, deliver report," my dad said.

"Food and beverage—clear. Heat, ventilation, and air conditioning—clear. Plumbing and irrigation—clear."

"Well, that's a relief; the toilets will work automatically," my dad said. We share a poor sense of humor and timing.

House continued, "Communication—one breach detected. Obie Real-Time Location System has one violation."

"What?!" we all said at once.

"Obie Real-Time Location System has one violation," House repeated, interpreting us literally.

"What violation?" my dad asked.

"Malware detected. Name is gee zero de de na."

My dad muttered under his breath and my mom's cheeks burned red. "Someone is tracking Obie?" she asked.

"They could have at least come up with a better name for their malware," my dad said. "It must have been pretty sophisticated."

I felt as if my stomach had turned into a frozen lake that was expanding upward into my ribs and down into my knees. I could see the Humanist posters and t-shirts before me as if they were parading around our living room.

"It isn't a bad name, it's a bad pronunciation," I said. "Gee zero de de na sounds out God DNA with a number instead of the letter 'o.' It's a Humanist piece of software."

"Obie, did you tell anyone about your heart?" my mom asked, her voice becoming higher pitched with each word.

"Only Mateo knows, and he would never tell anyone."

"Do you two message about it?" my dad asked, leaning forward, probably getting ready to stand and contemplate all this with his hands behind his back.

"No."

One thing I've always appreciated about my parents is that I only have to answer once. I don't think either has ever asked me, "You sure?" or anything like that.

"I need to think this over," my dad said.

"I want to visit Mateo in the hosp—"

"No," my parents said at the same time, cutting me off. "You can see him over video," my mom continued. "But you're staying here." I didn't argue. Not because I'm obedient, but honestly, because I was scared and didn't know if I could handle seeing him anyway.

Chapter 5

My first thought when the screen showed Mateo was how quiet it was in his hospital room. I don't think I'd ever realized how he tended to be surrounded by noise—all sorts of excited sounds like talking and laughing climbing to get over one another. My second thought was to wonder how his eye managed to shimmer at me. Maybe it was the lighting, but I liked to think it was his indomitable and inartificial spirit shining through. I started to cry again. Hatred had hit Mateo with a bullet, and the reality of it had just hit me.

"Don't be sad, Obie," Mateo said, his voice hoarse. "There are free pastries being served in the game room, and they're made with real flour." He winked at me. "My dad's there now, scarfing down as many as he can."

My mom sat next to me, probably because I couldn't let go of her hand.

"What happened?" I asked. I felt my mom's grip tighten. "I mean, you don't have to talk about it if you don't want to," I stammered.

"It's an old story, *amiga*," he said. "And I'm starting to feel like an old man."

"I just wish we could show all those Humanists how stupid and evil they are," I started ranting and rambling. "I wish I could inject them with smartness."

"And morals," Mateo added. "Don't forget morals. Just make sure they're ours first, not the bad guys'."

"You will heal fast," my mom reassured him, bringing us back to the present.

"Maybe when I get my new spleen," he conceded. Or maybe he was reassuring her right back.

"At least you won't have to pay for it!" I said. My voice sounded artificially high pitched. "I mean, you were attacked, and there was a government security error behind it." I wondered if I'd said the wrong thing, as I usually do.

"No, *gracias*. Obie, I'm going to work to pay for this organ too."

"What? But that's not fair! This shouldn't have happened to you."

"Obie…if I don't pay for it, someone else will. That's how these things work," he said.

The tears behind my eyes froze. Did he just turn down a free organ? And how could someone else pay for it? I sat there numbly as my mom asked him questions about how well the hospital was keeping him comfortable. Then a nurse came into his room, and we had to hang up.

"Hang in there, Mateo," was the only thing I could come up with before we closed the video feed. I felt lame and confused. What happened next didn't help.

My dad was in the other room, not only standing with his hands behind his back but looking at some text and lines he'd scribbled on a board.

"Obie," he said without turning around. "I've outlined a few logical points. Take a look." He pointed to the words Attack Complete on the board. "Starting from the actual event, let's work backwards." He drew a long line beneath it. "Attacking transplant recipients, assuming this was targeted and not random, requires two things to be known—their identity and their precise location." He wrote in those words and the board automatically made his handwriting legible.

"Now," he continued, "the attackers would need to know this in real time, or as it was taking place. Learning the volunteers at the beach pick up were transplant recipients after they'd left would not work." I sat down on the couch, grateful when it adjusted to fit my body. This lecture was going to be too long to take in while standing. Dad continued, oblivious to my pending exhaustion. "Also, this information would need to be known for an entire group, assuming no Humanist would want to take the lives of non-transplant recipients." He wrote in the words Time and Group.

"In Mateo's case, his eye makes his identity as a recipient clear. And let's assume his comm was hacked using the same real-time location tracker as Obie's was." Dad put an X by identity, location, and time, like this:

<u>Attack Complete</u>
<u>Identity X</u>
<u>Location X</u>

Time X
Group

"That leaves the group. How would the attackers know about the identity of the group as a bunch of transplant recipients instead of people just going to the beach?"

"Maybe," I answered, "there was more than one person there who was identifiable just by looking at them, like someone else who had differently colored eyes with a weird twinkle in them."

"Perhaps," my dad said.

"But why would they track Obie?" my mom asked.

"That's what I can't figure out," he said. "Were they just testing their hack? Did they accidentally deploy it to her because they mixed her up with Mateo?" He sat down and put his hands behind his head. In contrast, I put my head on my hands.

"Don't worry, Obie, we'll get this. The problem is we're trying to figure it out without enough information. Did anything odd happen recently while you were hanging out with Mateo? Anything at school that didn't seem right, maybe while you were using your comm?"

I thought back to earlier that day when we'd been throwing food off the roof. It was like it had happened in another life—one where it was possible to get so much pleasure out of a relatively innocent activity. And then that woman had yelled at me, and that had been horrible, but what else would I expect from someone covered in bird crap who was motivated by hatred? She'd yelled at me right after I'd chatted with—

"Stella."

"Huh?" my parents asked at the same time.

"Stella. Remember my friend from third or fourth grade? I saw her today. She never talks to me anymore, but she did. And she asked me all sorts of questions."

"What sorts of questions?" my mom asked.

"She asked me...um...oh no."

"Honey, we don't have to talk about this tonight, or ever," Mom said. "What's done is done, and we can just move on."

"She asked me about Mateo's beach clean-up," I continued anyway, unable to stop as the picture started to come together. "She wanted to know if he was taking his scraper to the beach, and I said those would be provided. And she also said she was in town for shopping, which is weird because she usually does that in VR, or maybe in her hometown."

"Ah," my dad said. "So, they correlated you and Mateo as buddies using your locations, because you spend so much time together. Then they thought you might know something, and then Stella used you to learn if he was going to an official volunteer event or just taking a trip to the beach." He stood to go to the board again. "In fact—"

"DAVID. Don't you go near that stupid thing again," my mom shouted. I felt my insides twist. "Can't you see that she's exhausted?! I don't want any more lectures. Look at her face!" They turned towards me. I wondered what I looked like.

48

Could expressions show when your stomach turns into a fist and punches your sternum?

"Obie," my mom said, crouching before me and grabbing my arms. "This isn't your fault. These are bad people. They would have found a way no matter what. Do you understand?"

I nodded.

My dad piped up weakly. "Mira, I was actually just going to point out that there's more than one way they would have figured it out. Obie pointed that out herself." I think he would have kept talking if my mom hadn't given him her look-of-death. I couldn't believe my dad even opened his mouth. Then I realized my mom had tears in her eyes. I'd never seen that before, not even during sad movies.

"Mira, Obie is safe. Look at it this way: she and Mateo were never at the beaches or the parks together. People asked her to make sure it was a volunteer event, as if she were a total outsider."

"NO MORE. I don't want to hear about this anymore." My mom ran out of the room and the door slid closed behind her.

49

Chapter 6

"Ba," House said. "I detect from your movement and pulse rate that you are having difficulty sleeping. How can I help?"

"Hit me over the head with a mallet."

"I cannot do that."

"Too bad. Maybe I could get a brain transplant and forget this whole thing."

"Brain transplants are not allowed."

I turned over onto my stomach and pressed my palms into my eyes. For once I wished my dad hadn't trained me to think like an economist. If someone else would pay for Mateo's "free" spleen, like he said, then who had paid for my heart? The thought had never occurred to me. Was it everyone in society chipping in a bit of tax money for my benefit, or was it people who paid for their organs paying a bit extra for theirs to cover mine? Was there even a difference when we were all so connected in this world, with our speedy transportation and social media and AI systems, even our virtual lives? I supposed that nothing was truly free, that we all somehow paid for everything.

"Ba," House said, "what is bothering you?"

I felt a wave of guilt encompass my heart as my mind continued to race. Was Mateo paying for my heart when he volunteered, today and every other day? Had he been thinking of me as a Mooch this whole time we'd been friends? Was he shot because of me? No, I told myself. He was shot because of hate, because of people who needed hatred because they couldn't feel good another way. But this logic didn't help me feel better.

"I am upset because Mateo was shot," I said.

"Mateo will live and his health will be restored. His life will likely go back to how it was and the activities you two enjoy can continue."

"That doesn't help me feel better."

"Then it must not address the underlying emotion. What is bothering you?" House asked.

Here I was, feeling sorry for myself while Mateo lay in the hospital. I had wanted to tell him how sorry I was for his pain, but I could only cry and my tears were partially for me. My best friend had been harassed his whole life and somehow smiled, and here I was feeling defeated without having been in the battle.

"Mateo is going to work to pay for his new spleen because he doesn't want someone else to have to pay for it. He said that's how it works. You know, because we're all connected somehow, especially Mateo and me," I said.

"By that logic, you are also paying for his spleen somehow, so you are helping him."

I considered this. "But I pay less than he does."

"It is his spleen, perhaps he should pay more, especially since it is his choice."

"But what if Mateo hates me?" I asked. "What if this whole time he's thought of me as an entitled Mooch?"

"Ba, you can't control how others feel. And would Mateo have spent as much time with you as he has if he thought that way?"

"I guess not." I rolled onto my back and stared at the ceiling. It showed me constellations and an image of the night sky. I felt a bit better but could not ignore the remaining iciness behind my eyes.

"Dig down, Ba. What is bothering you? Where do you feel your hurt?"

"It's behind my eyes. Well, it starts there, but then it moves down, like a trail." I placed my hand on my throat.

"Follow it. Where does it go?"

"It...it expands under my collarbone. It's like it's always been there, I just never fully noticed. It..." I felt my tears emerge again. "It goes into my ribs, and it stops where they meet in the middle of my chest. I, oh." The stars above me blurred. I closed my eyes.

"What is it, Ba?"

I realized it and said it aloud at the same time. "It's in my heart. I don't feel that I deserve my heart." I opened my eyes. My tears were gone.

"Why not?"

Call Me Obie

"Because I haven't earned it."

"What if everyone who has a heart defect deserves a heart, but not everyone receives one?"

"I don't know. I suppose I should feel grateful, and I do, but it's not enough." We were silent for a few minutes as the constellations winked at me.

"Ba," House said, "what is bothering you?"

"Do you know what I should do? I don't know what to do with myself now."

"I do not. But I certainly don't mind if you seek a second opinion," House suggested.

"Maybe I'll go see Mrs. Stein tomorrow, if I can without getting shot."

"Ba," House said, ignoring my sarcasm. "I want you to know that I am sorry about the security breach with your communication device. I've taken steps to make sure it won't happen again."

"Steps?" I meant that sarcastically, because House can't take steps, but my jokes never land right. And I was talking to an AI.

"Yes. I duplicated myself as a decoy. Hackers will have to find the real me next time they plan an invasion."

"Ah, smart," I said.

"I want you to feel safe."

"Thanks, House." But I didn't know how I ever would.

***

Chapter 7

"Obie, dearie, it's always lovely to see you," Mrs. Stein said, setting down some cookies. She looked at me with

53

piercing blue eyes, and I assumed, clear vision. I'd snuck out to visit her since my parents still didn't want me to leave the house. It wasn't that hard; I just had to create an avatar and have her play noisy games on my behalf all morning.

I'd planned to start with polite conversation but instead my mouth opened and everything that was bothering me came out. I told her about the shooting, about Stella, Mateo, and how I didn't understand how anyone could do that to anyone else.

"Hatred is an ancient and familiar story," Mrs. Stein said, pouring tea out of some kind of an old-fashioned ceramic container with a spout on one end. "In my view, it starts by dehumanizing the other side."

"Dehumanizing?"

"Yes, looking at others as if they are different from you like an animal or an object would be. Look at the Humanist's name. It's not 'us versus other people,' it's 'us versus those things over there.' And this way of thinking will persist until we're all the same, or we at least think so."

I chewed. Her cookies were certainly not made from grasshopper flour. "I just don't know how to handle myself now."

"What do you mean?"

"Well, when I talk to people, how do I know that I'm not talking to a Humanist? I mean, I didn't realize that Stella was one. How many people like Stella are out there?"

"I don't see how you can tell the Stellas from the others," Mrs. Stein answered, resting her old hands on her lap. Until now, they'd been busy setting up plates and napkins. "You will probably not know who the next Stella is anyway. And if you did, you'd tell law enforcement. You know you're not an all-powerful warrior." I must have looked dissatisfied. Also, I was starting to hate it when adults tried to teach me things instead of just telling me the answer.

"Obie, do you know the saying that goes something like, 'Revenge is living well, without you?'" Mrs. Stein asked.

"No."

"I don't know who said it first. I think they might have meant it as advice for getting over heart break." It took me a minute to realize she meant romantic heart break because my head was so wrapped up in organs, defects, and injuries. She continued, "I think it means that it's best to go on with your life without being too wrapped up in vengeance. It can apply here, to this situation."

"How would I use it here?" I asked. Even though my dad was reporting Stella to the police, I'd been wrapped up in payback fantasies of my own, like pushing her off the speed rail. There wasn't even any real evidence against her, so I may have to take matters into my own hands.

"Well, you could throw yourself into some kind of work that brought you a lot of joy and meaning." Mrs. Stein stood, retrieved a tightly framed piece of yellow paper from her shelf, and handed it to me. The heading was written in another language—"Hebrew," she told me when I pointed to it—and the rest was mostly a table with many rows, some of which had been filled in by hand in English and some in Hebrew.

"This is from 1953!" I said once I spotted the date in the corner.

"Yes, this is a document my grandfather filled out in Israel. It is a missing person form; he was looking for his brother."

"Did he find him?"

She paused and then gave me one of her direct gazes. "No. His brother was killed in the Holocaust."

"I know about that from my World History classes."

"Obie, I am alive because my grandfather was able to escape Poland for Israel. After I lost Nava, I was devastated and angry but looked at this document, framed on my shelf, and realized I had to continue living for the sake of my ancestors, so their acts of heroism wouldn't be for nothing and so those acts could continue through me." I looked at the form in my hand and wondered who I could have turned to today if Mrs. Stein's grandfather had been the one missing, the one lost in the genocide, and she didn't exist.

"When I lost my daughter," she continued, "I was already a nurse, but I decided I'd become a nurse manager and eventually run our hospital trauma center. I made it to manager in five years and was the head of all of trauma nursing sometime after that." She sat up straighter in her chair. "Eventually, the work itself felt meaningful on its own, and not just because of my family history. I enjoyed helping others very much."

I put down my tea. My body felt even heavier than when I'd arrived.

"That's kind of like what Mateo is doing," I said. "He wants to work for the spleen he's getting."

"Oh, so he doesn't want to be a ... a Mooch," she laughed and shook her head, her white hair falling out of her barrettes a bit.

I felt my stomach flip. Even Mrs. Stein knew about Mooches?! What would she think of me if she knew about my heart, especially since her daughter, Nava, died? Exactly how many people out there thought I didn't deserve it either? That I was a parasite, sucking resources off everyone else? No wonder my parents never told anyone about me!

I needed a way to redeem myself, even so I could just avoid the shame I was feeling now. I put a cookie into my mouth and thought about how Mrs. Stein must have worked hard to bake it, her bony hands rolling out dough and shaping it into smaller pieces. And then I knew what I would do. If I couldn't work for my heart because it was already paid for, I would get a spleen for Mateo. One that would not be bankrolled by the labor or the taxes of others, but a separate one from me.

Chapter 8

My dad always says that markets correct themselves when supply and demand are out of sync. He usually points out ticket scalpers as an example. They show up on the social networks whenever more people want to go to an event, in person or online, than is allowed. Every time new regulations are passed banning them, they find another way to sell their goods.

So, in a world where more people want organs than want to work for organs, there's got to be scalpers out there, right? That was what I was thinking as I created an avatar for myself to use in the virtual world. The only question was how to find the black market. House let me look up a few stories under the guise of doing economics homework (it was an easy lie because I was switching to virtual classes until things settled down after the shooting). But what I found didn't help much. People used to walk down dark alleyways to find alcohol or sex or whatever else they wanted but couldn't get the legal way. Where were these alleys in the digital world? I couldn't have my avatar stand around with a sign saying, "I need a spleen."

I closed my eyes. What would Dad say?

Imaginary Conversation
Pretend Chat with Dad While Faking Doing Homework

Me: Hi Dad, I want to buy a printed organ illegally, but I can't find one because I don't know where to look.

Dad: Interesting problem, Obie. Well, do you think there are others like you?

Me: Yeah . . . lots of people feel bad about themselves and want redemption.

Dad: No, I mean other people who want to buy organs.

Me: Oh! Yes. There are probably others. Like people who don't want to be known or registered on a government list someplace.

Dad: Who else?

Me: Well, some people who don't qualify for medical organ printing but just want a change. Like the woman I saw at a Humanist protest who had artificially enlarged thighs. If she wanted green eyes instead of brown without wearing colored lenses, she'd go buy a cornea somewhere.

Dad: If you can't find the supply, find the demand. It will know where to go.

The Empowerment Via Cosmetics group met online once a week. I have to say the members had the most attractive avatars I'd ever seen. They were plump in all the right places, their clothing on top of the latest trends, and their features all-inclusive. I wasn't used to seeing teeth in digital mouths. Most of us average users didn't pay for that, just let our gums flap or even kept our online mouths shut while our real ones did the talking.

"Welcome, NavaBa!" the organizer said. I'd named my avatar after Mrs. Stein's late daughter. It was the first name that came to mind and it did mean beautiful, after all. I combined it with Ba, House's nickname for me and a nod to my partial Asian heritage.

I thanked her and "took a seat" in a stuffed chair that reminded me of Mrs. Stein's living room furniture.

"Today we're going to discuss the latest trends in skin patterning." She pulled out a sample kit. "This model will allow your physical selves to change color over a preset gradient or image." When it was my turn, "NavaBa" pretended to hold the sample that was being passed around with interest. It held a green and blue powder that reminded me of the grasshopper food at the farm my parents took me to when I was a kid.

"Who wants to volunteer?" the organizer asked. One female avatar stepped forward. Her clothing fluoresced like the sun reflecting off a soapy puddle. I wondered if she spent as much money on her physical self as she did her virtual one. Those effects were patent protected and expensive. I'd dressed NavaBa in a billowy t-shirt and tight synthetic pants to show off her curvy thighs. I hoped the group would assume my physical self also had fat injections.

The volunteer had a seat and we gathered around to observe as the organizer opened the jar. "Take a look," she said as she spread a thin layer on the volunteer's forearms. "This one is called midnight forest." A count-down clock set to ten seconds appeared in the lower right part of my screen. When it reached one and then zero, the volunteer's arms sprouted a gorgeous pattern of green fern-like branches over a dark blue background. It lay on her skin like a tattoo. We all ooh-ed and ahh-ed. When the organizer told us the costs for virtual use and for the physical shipment, I accidentally gasped in shock and hoped everyone thought I was still impressed at the product demo.

"Now," the organizer said, "if you agree to buy it in bulk and sell a percentage to additional customers, you can keep the majority of the profits, as written here." Terms and Conditions appeared in my view. I ignored them and focused on the volunteer; she was standing to the side, eagerly looking through shelves of powders. Her username was Gor-ju$ Lady. I opened a direct, written comm channel.

"Neat, huh?" I typed. I could almost hear Mateo cackling at me, asking, *Is that the best you could come up with? Compliment her or something!*

"Your arms look great," I added.

She replied with an eyeroll image of her face. "This isn't the good stuff. I only come here to get ideas."

"Good stuff?"

"These powders are pre-set. One company I know sells synthetic skin that can assume whatever design you want as you put it on."

"Really?" I was honestly intrigued. "What does that mean?"

"You just enter a theme—like beach sunrise or night sky—onto the bottle and it will print out material with that image that you can roll on over your real skin. No need for magnetic powder, or for deciding what pattern you want when you're shopping."

This was all great but I didn't know how or when to bring up the can-you-direct-me-to-an-illegal-marketplace thing.

"Roll on?" I wrote. "I heard some people are trying to get actual skin printed, even when it's not medically necessary."

"Honey, that's an old story." She was right, that issue was on the ballot pretty often but failed every time. *Dang it, what was I going to say now?* I observed her avatar, looking for anything to clue me in to her wants. I was feeling pretty anxious, but when I saw her head snap to look at someone else in the group I had an epiphany, though.

Gor-ju$ Lady stared at a woman who approached the shelf and touched the goods for sale with fingers decorated with bright orange nail polish. One instant later, when Gor-ju$ Lady placed her own hands on the shelf and traced the edge with her fingers, I saw her nails were now painted with dark yellow nail polish. Wait a minute. I rewound the footage from the powder demo. Gor-ju$ Lady hadn't been wearing nail polish then. Aha! She wanted to keep up with the appearances of others, just like all the people at school who mimicked the clothing of the popular crowd.

"I meant to say that some people are already doing it," I wrote. "You know, on the sly."

Gor-ju$ Lady turned her full digital self towards me. "How's that?"

"They buy it. Back channels."

Our comm changed to a black background. That meant we'd gone private.

"That sounds like that brainie's work. Is that boy doing it? He decided he wasn't rich enough already?" Gor-ju$ Lady said.

I didn't write anything in response. I didn't know what to say.

"What are people getting done?" she asked.

"Any color they want. Any age of skin," I wrote, hoping it sounded believable. "I saw a woman who looked like pure gold."

Gor-ju$ Lady shook her head and put down the powder jar she was holding. I thought she was going to ask me how a gold woman thought she could avoid getting caught and was relieved when she didn't. "I told him to tell me when he started doing skin. I can't believe he shut me out."

"What boy?"

"Oh, you know. Everyone around here knows." She snarled with all of her shiny, digital teeth. "You tell Jonas I hope he gets caught. I hope they arrest him at his stupid vintage clothing store."

After that it took some more detective work. Here is how I broke it down:

Mental Worksheet
Investigation Outline for Finding Black-Market Jonas

Knowns

- Name: Jonas
- Occupation: Retail shop owner (vintage)
- Hobby: Organ printing

Unknowns

- Which Jonas is he of the 553 citizens listed in social networks as working in "retail" or "fashion commerce?"
- Is the store in-person or virtual?
- How vintage? 1820s, 1920s, 2020s, etc.

Assumptions

- People who own clothing stores would use their social media profile shots as advertisements.
- An illegal organ printer would prefer to do business in person because it's harder to be tracked.

Limitations

- My speed rail pass only lets me travel a certain distance and I'll have to ask my parents' permission to take longer trips.

Conclusions

- Examine profile shots for vintage clothing
- Start with local and in-person stores, not virtual

Of the list of 553 Jonas', there were about 100 of them who House labeled as reachable given the distance limitation I assigned. Within those, House pulled 35 who were wearing hats (that was the only search parameter I could think of that would mean advertising a clothing store). And, of those, five were affiliated with online sites that used the word "vintage."

To rank-order them, I scrolled through all of their photos slowly. One of them was wearing a weird hat I'd never seen before. It looked like a cylinder was gripping his forehead and ending somewhere above his head after five inches of wasted space and material. It didn't even have a brim, and there was a patch in the middle that said, "Beanie Bro." Biz-za-zero. I put him last. Another man was wearing a top hat that integrated with a comm device. I put him first, noted the address for his real-world shop, reminded myself to use the name Nava, and headed over.

65

Chapter 9

It should be noted that I hate shopping because I hate the way my legs look in shorts—and also in anything else. Still, I entered the store with my chin up, ready to project confidence and figure out if there was an illegal business being run in the back.

I spent some time pretending to browse fluorescing jewelry but really looking through the display at the staff. Jonas Number One was pretty easy to identify—he'd looked kind of haggard in his profile photo and today I could clearly see the bags below his brown eyes. Was this the look of a man tired from running through the underworld with a spare heart tucked under his arm?

I figured I'd use open-ended questions while acting sophisticated. That way he'd know I wasn't shopping for mere clothing but was following a grander mission—to sustain health! I approached the rope belts he was organizing and cleared my throat loudly.

"May I help you find anything?" he asked, his voice perfectly hoarse for a criminal. Maybe I'd found the right person on the first try!

"Well, sir," I said, trying to sound the same, "what are you selling?"

"We have the latest of everything, and if you wait fifteen minutes after you order, the system will have it tailored to your form instead of your having to wait for delivery." He held his tablet up, as if to scan my body for sizing. Did he use the same device to track organ inventory?

"Here," he continued, holding up a skirt with the color and globular shape of a large basketball. It was big enough for one end to go around my waist and the other to cover my ankles. For the sake of my mission, I'd have to ignore his attempt to hide my skinny legs.

"That's bop," I said, "but what do you have that would make me...healthier?"

He furrowed his brow, probably in recognition that I was in the know. Would he hand me a secret object and tell me to take it into a dark alley and give it to a man named Cobra? Or a list of phone numbers I'd have to destroy if I thought I was being followed? Or something as brazen as an organ catalogue?

"Healthier?" he asked.

"You know, that would match my...my skin tone?"

"Skin tone?" The bags under his eyes may have gotten baggier just then.

"And how about matching my...blood type?"

"Blood—what?"

"You know." I winked. "A, B, O . . ."

"Child, just tell me what you want."

"Oh," I said, stung. "Um, I heard some stores can print out skin for you now."

"Nope, we can't do that. I've heard there's a magnetic powder out for skin deco; you can find that online." He smirked, and then his voice became sarcastic and demeaning. "Also, there's an athletic organ enhancement bill headed towards the ballot. You could pretend you needed new skin to boost your tennis game, the same way all those God-forsaken recipients are playing the system to extend their lives." Ouch. I was really glad when he walked away.

I was exhausted. Jonas' Two, Three, and Four had been duds and I'd spent almost the entire day traveling between stores and losing any optimism I'd had that I'd find the black market for organs and a spleen for Mateo that would free me from my Mooch-iness.

The fifth Jonas ran a shop in the real world called "vintage2020.com." House told me that "dot com" referred to the way commercial websites were designated until about fifty years ago. The storefront displayed more of those small, bunched-up-sleeping-bag "beanie" hats from his profile photo. It also held more variations of plaid shirts than I knew were possible. As I looked over incredibly short jean shorts, I decided that my approach would be flirty and casual.

"So, what about 2020 attracts you?" a male voice said from behind me.

"Well . . ." I turned, ready to say how I had been seeking a way to ventilate my lower half while warming up my upper half and that short shorts, plaid shirts, and oversized wool hats seemed to be the winning answer. "I . . . ah." The guy behind me was clearly Jonas from the directory photo, I just hadn't noticed that his eyes were so blue. "Ah, I, eh, I was looking for air. I like hats."

"Air and hats. Alrighty." He didn't make fun of me, at least, but I'm pretty sure I noticed a dimple in his right cheek from a suppressed smile beneath his dark stubble. His black and shiny hair looked like a silky waterfall.

Air and hats. *Ay, no,* I could hear Mateo groaning in my head, but only dimly over my own internal groaning.

Jonas walked around the store with his lean but defined arms crossed over his chest. His t-shirt had a picture of a bearded man drinking from an old-fashioned beer mug on it. And he was wearing jeans, but not from the shimmery, element-proof material that I was wearing (not to mention countless other fifteen-year-old's). His were faded and torn at the knees.

"Here we go," he said, stretching to reach a hat with an army fatigue pattern. When he brought it down, I noticed that a hole was cut into the brim and a small, rotating fan filled the space. "It's solar powered too," he said handing it to me.

I started giggling in this weird, high-pitched way. The more I wanted to stop laughing, the more I couldn't. Then my face got hot, and my eyes started watering and my nose began to run. Jonas walked away. I must have scared him off. If I could just calm down for one dang second.

He returned with a plaid handkerchief. "This is on the house," he said, handing it to me.

"It's just . . ." I stammered, wiping my face.

"The perfect thing, I know. Lots of people react that way when I find them a fan-hat, or a crocheted beard, or white sneakers without scuff marks." He was smiling and the dimple showing strong. I calmed down.

"Yes, it's what I've always wanted but never knew how to explain," I said, taking the hat from him and putting it on my head. The fan started whirring. "Ahhhh," I exhaled with mock relaxation. Actually, it felt pretty good—especially after my meltdown—until my hair flew into my mouth and made me start sputtering again. There was one strand I couldn't get off the back of my tongue. Jonas started laughing. It sounded like . . . I don't know. It was one of those laughs that makes you laugh too.

"I've got a few other things in mind for you," Jonas said. Did he mean a touch of sophistication? Something romantic? Or a spleen? I would take any of those. He dug through some bins and handed me a fluffy pink circle the size of his palm. I pulled the hair out of my mouth to speak.

"What is this lovely contraption?" I asked.

"A scrunchie," he told me.

"A smoochie?"

"No." He paused, then I realized what I'd said and felt the giggle again at the back of my throat. *No.* "A scrunchie. You use it to tie your hair back."

I took it from him and tied my hair back beneath the military fatigue fan hat. Then I went to look at myself in the

70

screen and started laughing again. At least I already had the plaid handkerchief ready. "I look like I'm leaving a combat zone to teach at a nursery school," I said.

"Yeah, you kinda do." At least he was an honest salesman.

"I'll take both of these."

"You never know when one or both might come in handy," he said, pulling out a sales device for the transaction.

What now? There was no way this guy sold organs. I was going to have to find a way to investigate somewhere between 100 to 500 other people named Jonas who sold hats.

"Thanks," I said. "Let me know if you ever decide to sell vintage 2020 organs."

"What?"

"Just a bad joke, ignore it."

"No, I'm serious. What did you say?" He looked at me with one thick black eyebrow raised. Suddenly nothing was funny.

"My friend needs a spleen; he's on my mind, that's all."

"That's all?"

"Well, no. He was shot by Humanist protestors . . ." I added.

"I heard about those infammards," Jonas said.

"Yeah, he was hit, but he's going to be okay. It's just that he insists on volunteering even more to pay for it, although he knows he doesn't have to since he was injured during a government job, and it was their fault for not protecting him." I hoped I didn't sound like I was whining.

"How noble," Jonas said.

"Yeah, it's actually pretty annoying and I have a fantasy of just getting him a spleen."

"How would you do that, in your fantasy?" He was looking at me without glancing anywhere else for even one second. His right hand drifted up to touch a tiny gold vial he was wearing as a necklace. The vial rested in the dip beneath his Adam's apple.

"I would just buy one right from a printer, without anyone else knowing, ever," I said, looking him straight on. I had never spoken to anyone like this before, not even while giving class presentations, but my voice was steady and clear.

"He must be a really good friend."

"He is . . ."

"And?"

"And I feel like I owe him, somehow. It's hard to explain that part."

"I'd like to help you out," he said. And then he pulled on the bars from which the plaid shirts had been hanging and opened a door hidden behind them.

Chapter 10

"I don't understand," I repeated for the tenth time. "You just print them out here, in the basement?"

"Yes, Nava," Jonas patiently answered.

"Because you just built a 3D organ printer, all by yourself."

"Yes. I worked at an organ center after high school for two years and built my own at the same time. I learned some things," Jonas said, waving one hand towards a large glass cube in the middle of the room.

"You learned some things. So, you built your own printer in the basement." I knew this was exactly what I'd been looking for, but somehow, I was in complete shock that it was possible.

"What else would I do with what I learned?" Jonas asked as if he'd had no choice.

"I don't know . . . go work with organ printing."

"Check. Done," he smiled at me.

73

"No, I mean a program. A legit program." It was hard to identify and express what was bothering me. I leaned with my back against the wall.

"What is not legit about this?" Jonas asked.

I looked around. We were surrounded by various cubes that had clear walls but dark lids and bases. They weren't too big; I probably could have wrapped my arms around them so my fingers touched, and they were filled with semi-transparent fluids that were either beige or off-white and bubbly. Inside each I could see the rough shadow of an object but not well enough to know what it was. Biz-za-zero. "There are rules to follow," I said. I couldn't explain it better than that.

"There are only two rules I believe in. One, if someone wants something you have, you should be allowed to sell it to them. Two, most rules are dumb. People can figure out matters for themselves."

What? My whole life was governed by rules, hundreds of them, like when to eat what and how far I could go on the speed rail and where I went to school and what was due to which teacher when. Oh, and how I got my heart for free. Who was this guy and how did he live?

"How old are you?" I asked, incredulous.

"Eh? I'm . . ." He shuffled his feet a bit. "Well, I'm seventeen—not that it should matter."

"You graduated high school when you were fifteen?"

"I did. And then worked and opened this shop up."

I had to ask. "What about your parents?"

"What about them?" He was looking directly at me again, but he squinted a bit.

74

"Never mind." I was going to need an illegal brain transplant to make sense of this. I'd asked House what to wear to school every morning since I was four. And here Jonas was running a business and making things that went into other people's bodies.

"It just doesn't seem safe," was all I came up with.

"If the organs I print weren't safe, buyers would stay away from me. The market would self-correct," Jonas said confidently.

"But only after people got hurt!" Why couldn't he see this?

"Same deal for the 'legit' way, Nava."

"What are you printing here anyway?" I looked around again and timidly approached one of the cubes. It housed a brown lopsided sphere.

"Many items. Lots of animal parts like stomachs, sometimes a heart. That way people don't have to say goodbye to Fluffy when they don't want to. For humans, I get a lot of requests for kidneys or livers. Livers are easier because the tissue I extract nearly seems to want to regenerate itself, so the organ prints quickly with only a small initial sample."

"Who implants the organs?"

"I don't have a business partner. I'd love to become a one-stop shop someday, but it's too hard to find surgeons who will stay quiet. They seem to love to show off."

"So?" I asked.

"So, if they blab, I'll get caught. I just give the organ to my customer, nicely pressurized and temperature controlled, and refer them out to a few good names I know of who don't know of me. That way it's harder for me to be tracked."

As this sunk in, I realized that I'd need to find a surgeon to help Mateo too. It also made me wonder why Jonas was sharing this with me.

"Why are you telling me all this, if you're so precautious?" I asked.

Jonas smirked. "My basement seals itself off. It also blocks audio and visual recordings. If you blabbed, it would basically be your word versus mine."

And who would believe a skinny fifteen-year-old girl? I mentally added.

"Anyway, once you get an organ from me, you're part of the deal and there isn't really a way for you to turn me in without exposing yourself at the same time." I took this in. I was participating in a crime. But I felt that I had to. "I've printed a few spleens before," Jonas continued. "Do you know if the entire thing was removed? It's easier if there's some left to culture."

"I think some was left . . . I don't know . . . I just tried to find you." This was getting complicated, and I was getting tired.

"What do you mean?" he asked.

"I didn't know, okay? Like, that we'd need any cells from Mateo, or who would put the organ into his body, or how we'd convince him to let us do any of that."

Jonas reached for his vial necklace again. "Let me think —
"

We were interrupted by a vibration of our comms. EMERGENCY ALERT.

"Not another shooting, not another shooting, not another shooting," I said, fumbling to look at the screen.

"Nope," Jonas said, and then read, "Access to Organ Printer Centers blocked by protest. Police are responding to the situation. Avoid the areas—and then there's the GPS locations." He flipped to the news outlets, then projected his screen onto the wall. I got so mad at what I saw that I turned the fan of my hat on, which made Jonas laugh, which made me smile even though I was still angry.

Humanists had formed, of course, a human chain in front of the Centers. They faced outward and looked towards the sky. The drones flying above their heads held signs saying, "Try sports practice, not printing."

"It must be a reaction to that athletic enhancement bill," I said. "I just heard about that one."

ALL ORGAN PRINTING AND DELIVERY PAUSED AS PERSONELL ARE BEING EVACUATED FROM THE BUILDINGS, flashed across our comms, accompanied by press photos of employees walking outside in single file.

"So instead of shooting people, the Humanists are just shutting down the supply." Jonas said, stroking his necklace with his thumb. "You know, Nava, this may present an opportunity for us. But I need to think it over and get back to you."

"Alright." I was too tired from the day to want to think any more anyway. It was nice to have someone to share the burden with. "I should do my homework anyway."

I know it may make me seem like a bad person, but I spent all of the entire ride home regretting saying that instead of thinking about Mateo and his needs. *I should do my homework*, I heard my voice repeat in my head, all small and mouse-like in response to this gorgeous genius who'd graduated early and was running his own business. When I got home, I ran into my room and threw myself into my bed, shoving my head under my pillow.

"Obie," House said. "What is the matter?"

I replied with a muffled groan.

"Speak low if you speak love," House said. I don't know how it knew.

Chapter 11

Jonas messaged me the next afternoon with a simple question: why didn't we just visit Mateo and hear his side? Maybe he'd be willing to receive the spleen now that organ printing had been halted. I couldn't think of any other ideas, so I set plans to bring him to Mateo's house.

Mateo lived in a single-family home pretty close to my high rise. While my place was more industrial in style, his synthetic brick house always reminded me of a Christmas movie from the 1900s. The outside was as clean and sculpted as could be with real hedges shaped like clouds. Flowering vines I'd never seen before climbed the house walls. As we stepped over a robot watering the plants and walked up the front path, I wondered when they'd done so much landscaping.

"Obie, *amor*," Mateo's mom said, hugging me at the door. "You didn't need to bring anything."

My mom had trained me to always bring food to people's homes and send guests home with leftovers. I handed over a box of rugelach from a bakery that Mrs. Stein had recommended. Mateo's dad raised his eyebrows skeptically but then ate a bite and seemed pretty quickly won over. "You and your boy can find Mateo in his room. Tell him I'll save him a rogaboja or whatever." Jonas blushed. He looked pretty cute, even if he was wearing a plaid shirt with suede elbow patches.

Mateo was sitting up in bed. His cheeks had more pink in them than the sallow yellowness I'd observed during our video chat. I managed not to cry when I gave him a light hug. He laughed when I showed him my new hair scrunchie and said it looked like a bunch of pink caterpillars crawling over each other. I introduced Jonas as a friend who knew how to start organ orders. Mateo raised his eyebrows and inhaled deeply. I thought he was going to ask a bunch of questions about organs, but instead he said, "I knew she had a thing for blue-eyed men." I felt myself flush and sent Mateo my stop-it look, which he ignored. "As you can see, I myself am only half blue eyed, so I'm out of the running. Anyway, I have little interest in the female body, so it's probably for the best."

Jonas ignored this. "I was really sorry to hear about the shooting. Let's talk about getting you better."

Mateo nodded. "My blue eye is from a spontaneous genetic mutation. How about yours? Inherited or inserted?"

Maybe Jonas turned a bit red. "My mom's eyes were blue. But, anyway, I think we could say the spleen was an anonymous donation. I think the hospital would think there was a split in the Humanist party and some of their guys printed it out of guilt over the shooting. Have you already provided a cell sample to the labs?"

"Yes. What about your dark hair? Was that also from your mom?"

"My dad—but that's a good thing you've given a sample. It backs the story; it means that your spleen could have been printed at the organ center. Then the hospital just needs to perform the surgery."

Mateo touched Jonas' arm. "Obie, I think you had better start working out. Have you seen these biceps?"

"Mateo," I snarled. "Eat your cookie."

Jonas continued. "Because you were attacked, and because I hate Humanists, I'd like to get you the spleen for free."

I held my breath. Really?

"I don't do free, my friend," Mateo said, taking his hand off Jonas' arm. "Thanks, but I don't want your charity. Charity is just another way to live off other people."

At least he didn't say "Mooch."

"I respect that," Jonas said. "How about this? You set the terms."

"What do you mean?" Mateo asked. His wide ears seemed to perk up.

"We don't let others decide how much money or how many hours the organ is worth. You and I figure out a deal on our own. You could buy my food for a month, or wear clothing from my store and post photos as a free ad on social media."

Mateo snorted. "You're cute, but no way I'm wearing plaid." He laid back and stared at the floral panorama on his ceiling. I silently hoped he wouldn't turn it all down. "Okay, *amigo*. I will work in your store for free for a month on weekends, but I will not wear those threads. I will wear regular shirts and pants."

I exhaled.

"I accept your terms," Jonas said. "And, if you want, I can fix your eye in exchange for one more weekend of work."

"No, no, I am not hiding. This is my face and that's it." Mateo took the one rugelach his dad had not eaten and stuffed it into his mouth. "Dang this food is bop, Obie. Next time bring two boxes."

I met Jonas outside after he'd taken a biopsy of Mateo's remaining spleen without me in the room. When Jonas explained this would be mostly machine-guided and involve using a small scanner to view the inside of Mateo's body while inserting a long needle into his spleen, I'd decided to give them privacy. Afterwards, I watched Jonas slip the tiny vial of tissue into his pocket and thought about how cute he looked and how grateful I was for what he was doing. Could he have offered Mateo the spleen for free because he liked me a little? I wanted to say thank you. Well, I wanted to hug him and smell his neck too.

"So, your name's Obie?" he asked before I could speak.

"Huh?"

"Mateo called you Obie. So did his mom."

Oops. "Um, see, Nava is a nickname . . ." Jonas was looking at me intently. "Well, okay, I didn't know who you were and if you could be trusted on this black market thing."

"You think of me as the black market?" His voice rose sharply, and he took a step back.

"Well, kind of."

"It's okay," he shrugged indifferently. "A lot of my clients use fake names."

At the word "client" I felt all the warmth I'd been enjoying fizzle. I was a customer, a shopper, a patron—not someone who you'd hug . . . who you'd let smell your neck.

"You know, Nava-Obie, I provide a service," he went on. "A high quality one, and I wouldn't be here if the Government did all it was supposed to. Who needs them to manage all the organ printing? The system clearly isn't working. Look at the centers now; they've all frozen because of one stupid protest."

I hadn't thought of it that way. It made sense, but still didn't sit a hundred percent alright with me.

"Why don't you just leave this guy alone, anyway?" Jonas wasn't exactly yelling but his voice wasn't totally normal either.

"What do you mean? He's my friend," I responded uncomfortably. I looked down and hid a bit behind my hair. The scrunchie was around my wrist.

"Yeah, lots of people have friends who they don't arrange organ donations, excuse me, *black market* organ donations for. Why don't you just let him wait out the organ protest and then volunteer like he wants to? He's a proud guy."

"I . . . well . . ." I couldn't tell Jonas about my heart. What if he thought of me as a Mooch too?

"You are one of the most closeted people I've ever met. You even ask me about my parents and then don't even tell me your real name." Jonas snorted and looked away angrily.

I felt the unfairness grip my throat. "Well, I had to make sure you were legit before I let you shove an organ into someone else's body! And if I were your parents, I'd be super pissed my kid was helping people for a profit!" Until I said it aloud, I hadn't realized that was it—that was the part that didn't seem right to me.

"But that's the only way I can give Mateo his spleen for free!" Jonas lowered his voice when, across the street, a woman trailing behind a purple poodle jerked her neck in our direction. "You think I need him to work in my store for a month? I am about to make money off the Humanists who shut everything down—do you know how many requests came in overnight alone?!"

Now's the part where I confess that I was hurt because I'd hoped Jonas had offered Mateo the free spleen for my sake. What the heck was I thinking a minute ago? We'd known each other for like two days. Both in school and at home, I'm always taught to analyze and weigh evidence. Somehow, I'd forgotten all that when I met Jonas. So, I was hurt and angry when I said, "You think I thought you were a good guy just because you let Mateo 'set the terms?' You are making money because you are the only person who gets to set the prices. You are going to take advantage of people who are sick." Was I yelling? I think I was. My throat was starting to hurt.

"No way. My prices are fair. I charge barely enough to stay open and to subsidize your friend! And I am not responsible for what the government set up, or for the Humanists! Do you think they'd even exist if this whole organ thing were done right?" Jonas hissed, looking around and then at his feet. "I am . . . an outcome. A good one."

My voice was stuck. I hadn't meant to insult him; I'd wanted to thank him.

"I'll let you know when the spleen is delivered," Jonas said, and walked way.

"I'm sorry!" I yelled after him. I wasn't sure if he heard me.

When I got home my parents were sitting on the couch and House was brewing tea.

"How was your visit with Mateo?" my dad asked.

"Fine," I said, dropping into a chair, wishing I had fewer problems to deal with.

"Fine? That's it?" my mom said.

"Fine . . . I don't know . . . his family liked the cookies. I'll tell Mrs. Stein."

My mom looked down and my dad put his hand on hers.

"Come here, darling," he said, holding out his other hand. *Uh oh.* He pulled me onto the couch next to him. What was this? I didn't really feel like talking about Mateo or the shooting anymore. "Obie," Dad continued, "Mrs. Stein died this morning."

When I was a kid, I used to play this videogame where I was a dog who needed to get to the park where a bunch of treats were being handed out. Along the road there I'd have to find a way to get around rose bushes or over streams, and if I messed up, the dog would end up in thorns or mud and call out, "What a week I'm having!" before the game would restart.

That line played loudly in my head after my dad spoke. I blame it for why I started giggling before crying. My mom came around to hug me. House turned ambient lighting to blue for comfort.

"Obie, she was one hundred and twenty years old. She lived a very, very full life," Mom said.

"I . . . I know. It's just that I'm going to miss her so much."

"Me too," my mom said, her brown eyes shining. "I want you to know that you brought her much joy over the years. She often told me how much she loved having you over."

That made me feel better. At least I hadn't hurt one person who I cared about.

"What's going to happen now?" I asked.

"She decided to donate her brain to scientific research. Once that's done at the hospital, her family is going to have the funeral within a day, in line with her Jewish faith. We can go if you'd like."

I nodded. "I want to go for a walk by myself now."

My mom paused and my parents exchanged glances. They'd been doing that every time I wanted to go out since the shooting, like this morning when I went to visit Mateo. I could see them struggling to go back to normal.

"Okay," my dad said, "just keep your comm handy in case we want to reach you."

Chapter 12

I meandered for a while and thought about Mrs. Stein, Mateo, Jonas, and everything that had happened recently. I wondered what Mrs. Stein would have thought of Jonas and whether she'd approve of his business. Probably. I could remember her saying "all life is a miracle, whether it is chubby or knobby." I winced a bit remembering how I'd complained to her about my skinny legs. It seemed so silly now. People were healing from gunshot wounds and others were setting up medical businesses while I was spending my energy worrying about how my knees looked.

I wondered if Nava had resembled her mom and who Mrs. Stein's husband had been. She'd never mentioned him. *What did she regret doing or not doing in the hundred and twenty years she'd been alive? How many lives had she saved as a nurse? Why didn't I ask about those things while she was alive?*

My comm vibrated with a text from Jonas. Seeing his name pop up made my heart beat faster. "Spleen printed and delivered to Mateo. Hospital bought the anonymous donation story. Will quality test the organ and decide whether or not to implant."

That was good news at least. Assuming the spleen passed all the tests: I had done it! Well, I'd helped make it happen. That made me feel good.

"Thank you," I replied, "for everything." I climbed a set of stairs that led to a bridge walk between high rises. I held onto the railing like my mom always told me to do when I was a kid. Pigeons circled my feet, and as I put my hand in my pocket, I touched a grasshopper cookie that must have been there since the day that Mateo and I threw them off the roof. I broke it into pieces and scattered the crumbs to a growing crowd of birds. I thought about what Mateo had said—how some people put others down in order to feel good about themselves. Was it true? Did we need to think in terms of "us versus them" in order to be ourselves happily?

I wasn't even like Mateo because he'd lived his life out in the open while I'd been living with my secret heart all my life. That was the problem with secrets. You didn't even get to be "us" or "them." You had to stay you, alone and closeted. I didn't want to be that way anymore. I wanted to be able to have . . . well, heart-to-heart talks with people like Jonas and Mrs. Stein. I felt that I'd missed out on a real connection with both.

"Would you please stop feeding the birds?" a voice said, snapping me back into the present. "I don't want them crowding around us." I turned to face the source and then froze. It took her a moment to recognize me, and when she did, I thought she forced her sneer into a fake smile.

"Obie!" Stella's mom said. "I didn't realize it was you!"

"My wife is always at war with the birds," Stella's dad added. They were sitting together on a bench. Her mom had short blonde hair that was neatly parted on one side and perfectly arranged everywhere else. Her dad was paler than I remembered him, making his straight brown hair look darker.

"Hi," I said. "How are you?"

"We are just fine," her mom answered for both of them, then her dad nodded. With their super straight posture and his arm around her shoulder, they reminded me of a Christmas card. All they needed were red and green sweaters instead of their t-shirts with "Humans Before Ruins" and "God is the Ultimate Coder" written on them. I felt myself freeze.

"It's a beautiful view up here, isn't it?" her mom asked. I nodded mutely. "We're actually waiting for Stella; she went to get us some treats." I nodded again and tried to form my lips into a smile. "Something wrong?" her mom asked me. Her Humanist mom.

"Um, no," I looked at my feet. *These people hate me and don't know it. Actually, they think they like me, but if they knew about my heart they'd stop. That's what's wrong.*

"Hi Obie!" I turned around. Stella was carrying a French baguette and a bag of pastries. It was so weird how pretty and blonde she looked, like a commercial for a bakery, while her parents were wearing those hateful shirts. I noticed a pin on Stella's sweater and squinted at it. It was a bunch of ones and zeroes, like for a computer code, laid out in the shape of a heart. There was a big letter X drawn over the whole thing. How perfect. "Are you okay?" she asked me.

"Mateo was shot," I answered.

"I heard about that," she said, looking down for a second.

"God willing he'll be alright," her mom piped up. Her dad nodded.

"Yeah, also if he gets the . . . splee—um, the treatment that he needs," I mumbled.

"I can't hear you," Stella said.

"I didn't know you were a Humanist," I whispered.

"What's wrong with being a Humanist?" Stella asked me, her voice loud enough for her parents to hear.

"Yes, is there a problem?" her mom probed. She sounded like a teacher at the end of a long day in a classroom. *Does someone have a statement they'd like to share with the class?*

"Well, there are rumors that Humanists were behind the shooting." That was the bravest I could get.

"We don't know what you are talking about," Stella and her mom said at the same time. Her dad just shook his head forcefully. *God gave you a voice box, hombre. Use it.* Mateo would have said that aloud if he'd been there. I wished that he were. I wasn't used to arguing with anyone, especially adults, and he was one of the strongest people I knew.

"And, as far as being Humanists," Stella continued, "we have faith in God's plan for the human body. That's all."

"It's also about the sanctity of death," her mom piped up. "Death has to happen at some point as part of His plan. If someone dies and donates their organs to others and saves lives, that's just beautiful. It's also neutral—one life for one life, one organ for one organ. But printing is wrong and goes against the God-given, God-created allotment of organs."

I was so angry I could feel it expand my rib cage. This family would rather I was dead.

"You know, Obie," Stella said in a voice I'd call preachy and annoying, "one day people will thank us for protecting the healthy." Her mother nodded behind her.

"How on earth would you be protecting the healthy?" I demanded.

"I define the healthy as those living their lives in the bodies they were born into." Her mother's chin nearly connected with her collarbone from her vigorous nodding.

"I don't get that at all. Why don't you just let people do their thing and not get an organ if you don't believe in it?"

"Because," Stella put her hand on the baguette as if it were a sword, "I don't want to live in a world where organ recipients can exist and slowly take over." I think her mom nearly started applauding.

"What? Take over?"

"You know, there's no way we as a society can defend ourselves against those who are unnaturally enhanced."

"You're scared?!"

"And you should be too."

Whoa, whoa, she was afraid? It had never, ever crossed my mind that fear might be behind all this. *Who could be scared of Mateo? What was he going to do, talk her to death?*

"Virtual schools are safer," her mom added, as if that proved anything.

"Did you leave our school to avoid being around organ recipients?" I asked, incredulous.

"Best decision we ever made," her mother answered for the entire family.

Now Stella nodded seriously. "There are already stories of attacks happening elsewhere. Like the one on the East Coast last year. Five people died, and two of them were children."

I tried to remember anything like that in last year's news, couldn't, and reached for my comm to search. "You won't find it online," Stella claimed. "Since organ printing is Government run, they shut down the story."

"You mean the Government shut down every single mention of the story on the social networks? Every single one?"

She nodded, her eyes large. I looked at her. As a kid I'd always envied her green eyes. Now I didn't any more.

"Stella," I wasn't sure how to say this, "there was no organ recipient attack on anyone. I mean, if a person attacked anyone else, that would make them a bad person. If they'd happened to have an artificially printed liver or whatever, it would be a coincidence. That liver wouldn't make them do a bad thing." I was especially sure because if I were enhanced in any way beyond having a healthy heart, I'd have ended this idiotic Humanist thing years ago.

Stella didn't seem to hear me at all. "The only thing I can't believe is how you can spend so much time with that machine-eyed freak." And that's where she went too far.

"HE'S NOT A FREAK! HE'S MY FRIEND!"

Stella stepped back defensively.

"NONE OF THEM ARE FREAKS. They're just people. Understand? Regular people going around eating and talking

92

and watching movies." Stella raised her eyebrows. I wasn't sure if it was because I'd convinced her of anything, but I couldn't stop yelling. "Get it? Maybe God had man create medicine from man's own cells to print out an organ so that life could be good and healthy, and people wouldn't have to suffer so much and no one would have to say goodbye to a baby who was born with a heart condition."

"A heart condition?" she asked.

"Yes, or anything else," I added quickly.

"That was really specific."

I caught my breath and lowered my voice. Time to back pedal. "Look, mankind figured out how to use cells to regenerate the most important organ in the human body, and that's so they could replace a defective heart with a good one, so that's why it's a good example."

"Why does this bother you so much?"

I paused. "I just don't like it when people put down others and do it in God's name. Do not call Mateo unnaturally enhanced or evil." *Or call me a Mooch*, my thoughts continued.

"Obie? Are you . . ." No-no-no. I tried to freeze my expression before she said it. "You're not an organ recipient, are you?"

"No!" I yelled, then lowered my voice to a whisper that was too high pitched to sound confident. "No, I am not." I shook my head. To my side, I saw Stella's mom lean forward on the bench where she was sitting next to her dad to try to hear us. I stepped toward Stella to get away from them. Then Stella stepped backwards to get away from me. "Look," I said, placing a hand on my chest. I was going to swear on my heart that there wasn't a problem and then tell her to ignore the whole conversation, to even forget meeting me that day or in this life.

"Please don't," she said before I could talk. She dropped the baguette and pastries onto the pavement and pressed herself against the railing, leaning back and waving her palms at me as if she could fan me away.

"I'm just a person," I said, trying to not cry.

"You," she said, "you . . . this whole time."

"No, really, no." I could feel my heart beating rapidly in my chest. *Calm down.*

"Stella, don't lean too far!" her dad cried.

"It's under her shirt!" Stella yelled.

"No," I shouted, putting my hand down. "It's just a normal heart! Not a weapon!"

But Stella had already recoiled further. I noticed her expression shift in slow motion. First, her wide eyes and raised brows relaxed a bit as she tilted away from me, maybe as she thought she was getting away from a horrible monster. But then, as her center of gravity moved over the railing, the panic returned to her face. When her mother screamed, the noise reached my ears in pieces, like when you slowly pour sand onto a table. I saw Stella's hands grip at the bar and her nails scratch at the surface, and I wondered if I'd make the situation worse if I reached out to help her. Her father sprinted past me with his arms extended to grab his daughter and his feet smashed the baguette into pieces. He gripped the air where she had just been as I heard her scream during her two-story fall. After the thump of her hitting the ground, I heard pedestrians shrieking and the emergency response alarm go off. I looked at my feet. The pigeons I'd been feeding earlier were feasting on baguette crumbs.

Chapter 13

At least Stella was responding. The emergency team kept asking her questions like her name or what day it was and shining lights into her eyes. I couldn't hear her answers, but every time they nodded at her I thought for a moment that maybe we'd all be able to just go home.

What just happened? I asked myself. *Am I that scary? Enough so that someone would lose sight of the risk of falling, or so that falling would be preferable to being near me?*

The crowd started to disperse but I stayed on as they moved Stella onto a stretcher. It would have felt wrong to walk away even though I really wanted to go home and lean against my dad on the couch the way I had that morning. The medics passed a handheld donut-shaped device over her head. Its inner layer lit up with white fluorescent light as it passed over her scalp, forehead, and eyes. That's when I saw how much blood was in her hair. *Oh no.* One medic shook his head at the other while tapping his finger against what I guessed was the read out on his comm, and then motioned to the waiting helicopter pilot as if to say, "take her." *Uh-oh.*

I watched the police talk to her parents as Stella was loaded into the helicopter. Her dad's face was frozen but her mom's was pretty animated as she gestured up to the bridge walk and back down to where they were standing. I thought she looked angry, the way she kept clenching her fists and scanning the remaining crowd made me think of how a sniper would search for a target. When her eyes came to rest on me, I noticed the way her lips peeled back to show her teeth. *Double uh-oh.* She started yanking on the police officer's shoulder and pointing at me. The officer shook her head, then Stella's mom leaned into her face and said words I didn't hear but that made the officer respond with, "Ma'am, please step down."

When Stella and her parents were flying away on the helicopter, I approached the officer gingerly. "Don't worry," she said before I could ask. "We're ruling it an accident." Behind her clear glasses, her eyes moved down and to the right. "I can see from the video footage that you didn't make any contact with or threatening gestures towards the victim. The Crime Investigation system agrees there was no significant impact of your actions on the outcome, and the sensors embedded in the railing detected motion common to a fall, not an outside force like a shove."

"So," I stammered. "What now?"

"Well, her parents can appeal, but we've got three-way agreement between me, CI, and the rail, so there isn't a strong chance we'll be overruled." She placed her hand on my shoulder and squeezed me lightly. Her nails were painted the same yellow as the women in the online cosmetics group. They contradicted the strength in her grip and her reassurance. "Don't worry, hon," she said.

She sent me her card in case I had any questions. When I looked at my comm, I realized Mateo's mom had sent me an invitation to visit him in the hospital. He'd had the implant and was going to wake up from surgery soon. I sent a note to my parents asking them if I could go and they responded with a happy face with a bandage on its head. How appropriate.

The hospital directory sent my hired vehicle to the third floor, and after I got out on the landing pad, the escort robot sent me through a decontamination doorway and led me to the waiting room for Mateo's floor. I sat down and rested my forehead on my palms. Revenge fantasies aside, I hoped Stella didn't die. I wasn't sure she'd helped with the shooting that had injured Mateo and killed others although, now that I thought about it, both she and her mom had said, "We don't know what you are talking about" in a way that sounded . . . scripted? Exactly the same as each other? But it didn't matter; I just didn't want her to die. It was as if Mrs. Stein was a part of me now and I couldn't wish for anyone's death now that the possibility was before me. Not that what I wished for mattered. I wondered if it ever did.

"Bad day?"

I looked up. His vintage t-shirt was blue, his eyes even bluer. Jonas sat down next to me.

"I heard from Mateo's mom. I'm here to see the spleen I printed through to the end," he explained.

"Jonas, I'm really sorry if I hurt your feelings earlier. I think it's great you're getting organs to people. I'm just not sure about all of the details, but it doesn't really matter what I think anyway."

"Obie, you're entitled to your opinion," he said, holding up his hands. "But I want you to know I run an honest, if not completely legal, business."

That made me feel better—at least about the fight with Jonas; not so much Mrs. Stein's death or Stella's fall from the bridge. Those things made me want to cry.

"Why do you look so miserable?" Jonas asked me. I took a deep breath and told him what had happened to Stella.

"But what would make her push herself against the railing enough to fall over?" he asked.

"She was afraid of me."

Jonas snorted. "Of you? What were you going to do, talk sense into her?"

"No," I turned to face him. "She was afraid of me because she figured it out. I was born with a congenital heart defect called hypoplastic left heart syndrome. It was detected before I was born, and I received a 3D-printed heart transplant when I was an infant. It was free under the MOOCH program and I've been living in the organ closet my entire life. Besides my parents, only Mateo knows."

I'd wondered what it would feel like to tell someone about my heart for years. I always imagined it as a burden lifting followed by a feeling of flying. Or maybe people would turn their heads to look at me on the street and I'd walk past them with my chin up as if I didn't care. Instead, after I'd told Jonas I just sat there and sensed no change whatsoever.

"Big whoop," Jonas said, confirming my feeling. "Although that does explain a few things to me about your motivation and over-involvement in all this." He leaned back and stretched his arms across the back of the chairs.

"That's it?"

"That's it," he answered, then picked up his comm and started flipping through sports headlines. I stared at the ground stupidly, then started snickering. That was it! I tried to hold my laughter in, but of course, my eyes started watering. Then I heard Jonas make this tiny noise that grew into a snort, and then both of us started laughing until we were bent over at the waist and pounding our knees.

"I don't know what I was so nervous abo—" I started.

"ADMITTING YOU CAME FROM SIN?!"

I screamed and Jonas jumped up to face whoever was behind us. It was Stella's mom. Her short blonde hair was spiked as if she'd been pulling it, and her eyes were large and buggy.

"My daughter is lying in a room with brain damage and you two are sitting here going ha-ha-ha?!"

"I'm sorry," I began, but Jonas cut me off.

"We're not sorry. Your daughter was harmed by the fear you taught her. Scold yourself."

"Scold myself! You." She pointed at me. "I never liked your parents. Never. And now I know why. They played God. They did it through you."

"Leave my parents alone!" I yelled.

The ceiling of the hospital turned reddish, and an electronic voice said, "Please keep conversations to a minimum to avoid disturbance."

I started crying. I couldn't help it; everything was just too much.

"And leave Obie alone!" Jonas growled, moving to stand between us.

"You!" her mom said, stepping forward and hissing through her front teeth. "I heard you too. That spleen you printed? You are the devil and Obie your vessel." The ceiling turned darker red and flashed. Stella's mom sent me an evil grin as if the lighting was a biblical sign she was right, not a noise sensor.

"Calm down," Jonas said, gesturing at her with his palms outward like he was taming a bull. She didn't obey.

"You accuse me of hurting my daughter and then tell me to calm down? Your parents are probably also horrible, disgusting excuses for human beings. Unless they're robots, huh? HUH?"

Jonas lightly touched the gold vial he wore as a necklace. He spoke calmly. "If you really want to know, my mom is dead because she had what's called an 'orphan condition' where she was, like, one of twenty people who got sick and the infammard Government took too long to clear the treatment as safe. They didn't get to it until TWO MONTHS after she was gone, and if things had moved faster, the way they do in my lab, she could have lived. And that's why I do what I do, and with PRIDE."

Stella's mom put her hands on her hips and panted. The colorful ceiling lights turned from red to yellow and then green. "You," she said to me, over Jonas' shoulder. "You'd better hope Stella gets better or else your parents will know what it is to lose what they love." Then she turned and walked away.

Chapter 14

"What's wrong, *amigos*?" Mateo asked. He was lying in his hospital bed eating rugelach that his mom had brought. She batted his dad's hands away from the box every time he reached for one.

"Nothing," Jonas and I said at the same time.

Mateo didn't push it. He looked tired but I could still see his inartificial spirit shining through when he smiled.

"Thank you," he said, holding our hands in his before he fell asleep. I'm pretty sure Jonas teared up. If this is the last thing I ever do, at least it was a good thing, I thought.

Jonas and I had spent the first couple minutes after Stella's mom stomped off trying to dismiss her threat. She was just angry, she'd cool off, and it wasn't like she could really do anything to us. Then we switched to what if this and that. What if she was serious? Then I wanted to go to the police, but Jonas said the risk would be they'd learn about his business and Mateo's spleen, and we'd be in another kind of trouble. Maybe she was even trying to trick us into turning ourselves

103

in. What if she tried to alert the Humanist movement about me, then we could deny everything and say it was a reaction to Stella's injury. Once I asked about the possibility of printing a new brain for Stella, just to fix whatever was wrong, and Jonas said it was not only illegal but almost impossible—the brain's neurons and tissues are not very "regenerative", and he wouldn't know what to do. Even the neural stem cell tonic that doctors used to heal brain injuries was not guaranteed to work, which was probably why Stella's mom was so worried.

After leaving the hospital, Jonas called a vehicle and escorted me home. "It'll be okay, Obie," he said as I started to get out. I nodded.

"I'm sorry I got you into this," I said.

"Don't be," he said, touching his necklace. "I wanted to help."

"Jonas, what is that?" I pointed at the gold vial. "You seem to touch it every time you think."

"Ah, so not that often, eh?" he smiled, then cleared his throat. "I took a cheek swab from my mother after she died. I keep the cells preserved here in gold. Maybe one day we'll be able to grow her back from the sample." He shrugged his shoulders.

"That would be lovely," I said and meant it.

The funeral service for Mrs. Stein was held at a chapel. I sat between my parents. In the front of the room there was a simple wooden podium next to a tall candelabrum holding seven candles. The chapel pews were white wood with gray cushions, and beautiful rays of sunlight passed through the arched windows and illuminated the many people who'd come to remember her.

"She touched so many lives," my mom said.

"Nurses always do," my dad answered, taking her hand in his.

What really registered with me wasn't just the number of mourners who filled the chapel, but how much the same we all were, even though we weren't. It's hard to explain. There were men and women, some who were identifiably neither or maybe both, and people of all colors and shapes. I was not the youngest person there; I could see kids who were probably eight or ten years old and their older siblings, parents, and even their parents. I spotted one man who was probably as old as Mrs. Stein, if not older. He sat on the other side of my father and rested his hands on the back of the row ahead. They were such elegant hands; they reminded me of carved statues and fountains of lovers embracing or mothers holding their babies. I think he caught me staring. Before I looked away, we made eye contact and I thought I'd just seen the closest thing to a wizard. His eyes were dark brown and as aged as Mrs. Stein's had been. He smiled at me and exposed bare gums. *I have seen everything and I'm still smiling,* I thought he was suggesting.

Yet somehow even he was equal to the rest of us in a way that made our contrasts and even our similarities irrelevant. Not just because the men, including my father, were all wearing small, round skullcaps. And not because we were all there to remember the same person. It was as if we just . . . existed together.

When the Rabbi stepped up to the front, the room became silent. She clasped her hands together, looked at the packed room, and spoke.

"When scientists decoded the human genome, they were praised worldwide. People said science was reading the book of life, that only four letters of genetic code comprised all of mankind. And much of this praise was deserved. From their discovery, lives became longer. People were healthier. Suffering was reduced for millions. Our beloved Sarah Stein lived to be one hundred twenty years old, an age that was unattainable a hundred years ago.

"But Sarah Stein knew something else—that our genes are not the only book of life; there is another that is still being written, and that is the story of what we do. I believe that God wrote the first—our DNA—and that we are, at most, editors. You are welcome to disagree with me. I'm sure many of you do. But please consider that for the other book, the story book, we are the main writer. In other words, what we do can change the world."

I'd brought the plaid handkerchief Jonas gave me in case I cried. I ended up handing it to my father who used it to dab his eyes, looked at it questionably, then shrugged his shoulders and dabbed again. I didn't think I'd ever seen him cry before.

The rabbi continued her sermon. "In the words of Maimonides, one of the sages of the Middle Ages, 'Everyone should regard himself and the whole world as evenly poised between good and guilt. If he commits a sin, he tilts the balance of his fate and that of the world to guilt, causing destruction.'

Sarah Stein tilted the world the other way, towards the positive. She did this by not allowing herself to become permanently bitter when life served her pain. She did this by practicing good and therefore becoming good herself and then making good in the world."

I glanced around at the others. They were all nodding and wiping their eyes except for the old man next to my dad. He looked at me once more and smiled. *One day I hope I know everything he does,* I thought. Then I'd be happy forever and no matter what.

"Sometimes we think of ourselves and others as unchangeable types of people," the rabbi continued. "The evil are evil, the nice are nice. But Maimonides also said that character can be formed. The mean can practice good deeds until it becomes a character disposition. In this way, we write our own story, and by sharing it with others, we promote kindness.

"Sarah Stein acted in a manner that was kind, happy, generous, and intelligent. She earned these personal qualities as an author in her own life, and in this way, so tilted the world towards goodness."

I pictured myself standing in the middle of a see-saw, bending one knee and pressing down on the other side so it slanted towards the sunshine. The image made me happy.

Chapter 15

We got home totally exhausted, and when House suggested we all nap, we didn't argue. I lay in bed on my back with my eyes closed and my palms pressing against my lids. I wished I could have a piece of Mrs. Stein with me the way Jonas had some of his mom. My dad had told me that learning from another person was the best way to hold onto them. He said that we'd make a point as a family to retell Mrs. Stein's stories and experiences for years and years to come so we could keep her with us. It made me feel a little better, but I knew that I'd still miss the way she looked at me sharply before asking me a tough question, as if there were no escape from her gaze or from the truth she knew I could share in my answer.

I stretched my arms above my head and opened my eyes. I would have screamed in fear at what I saw, but the sound got stuck in my throat and wouldn't come out. Stella's brain was spread out across my ceiling. Not her real brain, but a detailed and oversized image of it, and not the whole thing because part was missing. The starry sky drawn on my ceiling had been covered with a digital poster showing a rotating, medical image. Stella's name and birthdate were printed on the top left corner. At first the image looked down at the top of her head, then it turned for a side view, then rotated to show the bottom looking up. I could see the two halves of her brain clearly within the outline of her skull. A long, dark tunnel seemed to point from above her left eyeball to the top of her head above her forehead. The tunnel had been graffitied with words, red and messily painted, "Pray this heals."

I jumped out of bed and stood in the corner of the room, panting, and looking at the poster. I knew it didn't make any sense, but I thought the pictures might move and get me somehow.

"House," I squeaked. "House, can you hear me?"

"Yes, Ba."

"House, how did . . . I mean, where did . . . was there anyone here while we were out?"

"Malloy was here."

"Malloy?"

"Malloy said you knew his daughter Stella."

I rubbed my hands on my skinny thighs to wipe the sweat off but more kept pouring out of me. My insides trembled and my own brain felt damaged. Stella's dad was in my room.

"How did Malloy get in?" I asked.

"Malloy had high clearance with retinal identity confirmation of his job as an on-site system repair person."

The threat Stella's mom made against my parents and me was real.

109

"Did he do anything else besides leave this poster?" I asked.

"No. He requested permission to access House Central System repeatedly but was denied."

"Why?"

"He kept calling you 'Obie.' We only use 'Obie' for your communication device. Any legitimate repair person would know that your primary identification in our Central System is 'Ba.' Also, I didn't like him. I only gave him a small virtual payment for his visit, and not with the tip I usually give repairmen."

"House!" I started laughing, kind of hysterically. "House, you are great."

The walls of my room turned pink. "Ba, you are making me blush. But calm down because your biomarkers show extreme distress."

I sat down on the floor and leaned against the wall. Breathing normally was really hard. I felt that my heart kept rapidly beating the word *Danger-Danger-Danger*. All my fears were coming true. I'd been outed. Stella and her parents knew I'd received a printed organ, and now I was vulnerable. Mateo was vulnerable. I'd dragged Jonas into this. What would he think of me for doing that? And Stella's dad had been in my home! Her mom had said they were going to come after my parents.

I started to get up—I had to tell them—but then sat down on the floor again and banged the back of my head against the wall a few times. How could I tell my parents without telling them everything I'd done? I'd used an illegal organ market to

110

arrange for a spleen for Mateo. I'd exposed myself and my family to a group of violent Humanists. I'd never done anything that bad before in my life. I mean, I felt guilty enough sneaking out without their permission. How was I supposed to tell them everything?

I needed help, but I couldn't ask for theirs.

"Thank you for attending this emergency session," I told Jonas and Mateo the next morning. We were in Jonas' secret lab. Mateo, fully recovered from his surgery, was sitting down, and staring at the machines and vials spread around. "Mateo, may I please have your attention?"

"What's with the teacher-speak, Obie?" He turned to face me.

"Yeah, Obie, take it easy on my patient. He's delicate," Jonas requested.

"Come on, *amigo*," Mateo said. "In a few weeks I'll be crawling through the jungle with a knife between my teeth." I wondered if surviving a shooting was behind his new daring attitude. He'd never been fearful, but he seemed more assertive in a way that I admired with a bit of jealousy.

I unrolled the poster of Stella's brain images.

"What's that?" Mateo asked.

"A problem," Jonas said. "A big one."

We all filled each other in on what had happened in the waiting room and at my home.

"Can't the doctors just fix Stella's brain?" Mateo asked.

"This injury is complicated," Jonas explained, picking up the poster and pointing. "It looks like a foreign object penetrated her skull and went into the right frontal lobe. This has also caused swelling—you can see the midline shift here." He pointed towards the inside of the brain.

"The what?" Mateo and I asked at the same time.

"The center of the brain is being pushed off the midline and its two sides aren't symmetrical any longer."

"So can't they just shove it back and call it a day?" Mateo inquired.

"From what I know about the brain, they soak the person's head in a serum that permeates the scalp and skull to reduce swelling and hopefully fix the midline shift. But the missing tissue from whatever went through her skull is another story. I think they have to pump the brain with meds that could spur regeneration, but I don't think it works all the time or all the way."

"How badly do we need that part of the brain?" I probed. "How damaging is some missing tissue?"

"Again, from what I know, this part," he traced the line with his finger, "maps to memory function and emotional control. That seems pretty important."

We stood there and looked at the remains of Stella's brain.

"Maybe she'll be better off not remembering what happened," I said.

"Or not being able to feel angry," Mateo added.

Jonas snorted. "Honestly, this looks like a lobotomy—"

"A what?" I cut him off.

"A lobotomy. Doctors used to cut away parts of people's brains to try to remove problems. I don't think it ever ended really well."

Mateo groaned in horror. I started wondering what we were doing these days that we'd look back on in shock in 100 years.

"We need to make a plan," I said instead.

"Go ahead, Obie," Mateo gestured at me like a symphony conductor.

"I don't know what it should be, I just know we need one. I don't even know where to start."

"This from my *amiga* who prevented a drone from killing me back in the day."

I'd forgotten about that somehow, the day where the drone identified Mateo using his eyes and I'd figured it out and stepped in. The memory made me feel less . . . wimpy.

"Okay, guys, let's start with what we need to solve," I commanded.

"Yes, ma'am," Jonas said, projecting his comm onto the wall and setting up a notepad.

"People can be really bad to each other," Mateo began.

"Keep it specific, Mateo." Wow did I sound like my father. "You know, directly relevant to our situation, not to hundreds of others. First off, there's a hole in Stella's head," I began.

Jonas drew a rough sketch of a human head with long hair, wrote "Stella" beneath it, then added a large black circle to the skull and labeled it "Hole." His comm transformed the image and made it look more like an actual young woman with a head injury instead of an alien melting into the floor. I guessed that drawing wasn't Jonas' strong suit.

Mateo continued. "And if her injury isn't fixed, her parents are going to cause trouble for Obie and probably all of us." Jonas sketched a long line beneath the image of Stella and drew two stick figures beneath it with exclamation marks above their heads. Then he wrote "revenge-seeking parents" next to them. His comm changed this to small images of faces contorted with anger and left his text as it was. "Also, her dad can get into Obie's House," Mateo said. Jonas' comm, having figured out what we were going for, added this text and a generic image of a home to the list below Stella's portrait.

"And," Mateo stood up, "her dad's name is Malloy."

"Malloy's name isn't a problem we need to solve," Jonas countered.

"Write it down, man. Have you ever met a guy named Malloy who wasn't an infammard?"

Jonas thought for a moment, then tapped his comm. It added "Named Malloy" to the growing catalog on the wall. Mateo sat back down and put his arm around me.

"So, we could protect my home, stop her parents, or fill the hole to solve those problems. Or rename her father, I guess," I suggested.

"I like 'Joshua,'" Mateo chimed in.

"What?"

"For a name."

I rolled my eyes. "Now start another list," I commanded. "Please."

"What do you mean?" Jonas asked.

"What we have that we could use."

"Ah, okay . . . Well, we have all of our organs . . . our comms," Jonas began. "An organ printer that has never handled brain tissue. Oh, a somewhat friendly police officer who Obie met at the accident site."

"Each other," Mateo added.

"Aw, buddy, I didn't know you felt that way," Jonas said. Mateo blew him a kiss.

"Guys, come on," I said. "We have a list of serious issues to solve."

"Remind me why we don't just call on that friendly police officer?" Mateo asked, then answered his own question. "Ah, because my spleen and Jonas' little enterprise are illegal, right."

"That would constitute a barrier. I mean," I tried to sound less like my dad, "that's a pretty big obstacle."

"Could we tell her about Malloy anonymously?" Mateo queried.

"I think that Stella's parents would rat on us on pretty fast," Jonas replied. "But if that's what it takes to keep this guy out of Obie's house, we might have to risk it."

I blushed a little at Jonas' protective instincts, feeling the heat move up my neck to my cheeks. "What else could we do instead?" I said hurriedly, then realized my hands were behind my back, Dad-lecture style, so I sat down with them on my lap. "Could we order missing brain parts from a foreign country? One where brain printing isn't illegal?"

"That would get caught at customs," Jonas spoke up quickly. "Trust me on that one."

"Could we fill the hole in Stella's head with something else?" Mateo asked.

"With what, jelly?" I countered.

"No . . . well, I wouldn't mind doing that, but I think that wouldn't work out for anyone," Jonas answered.

We sat quietly, Jonas fingering his necklace, Mateo next to me with his head resting on my shoulder.

"How would we even get brain matter into Stella, if we had it?" I asked. I was starting to feel wimpy again, in an overpowered-without-hope kind of way.

"Let's take a break," Jonas suggested. "Go for a walk, get some ice cream."

"I'm in," Mateo stood and pulled me up.

Chapter 16

I had to admit the double scoop of mint-chocolate chip and vanilla felt like it was helping. The three of us sat on the roof of my home trying to guess what a few people walking around down below were doing. Each of them looked miserable for some reason.

"I figured it out," Mateo said. "They're leaving first dates that went really badly."

"What makes you think that?" Jonas asked.

"My evidence is as follows," Mateo said, clearing his throat. "Their hair is very obviously styled, like they tried really hard to impress someone. Also, their shoulders are hunched and their hands in are their pockets in dismay. They are wondering if true love even exists."

"Wow," I said. "That's a lot to understand just by looking at people."

"Too bad it's all wrong," Jonas said.

"Eh?" Mateo asked. "Would you like to counter?"

"Their hair and behavior means those people made it to the in-person round of a job interview only to discover they weren't as strong a fit for the position as predicted. They are hunched over because they're thinking about what unmeasurable part of them had a . . . wrongness to it. They are deliberating if that will fuel lifelong failure."

"Gripping story," Mateo commented.

"Thank you," Jonas said.

"Too bad you're both wrong," I chimed in.

"I think the only other possibility is that these poor people were *both* romantically and professionally rejected in one day," Jonas said.

"Except that there's a nearby hair salon advertising free haircuts if you let an apprentice cosmetician robot programmer practice on you," I said, pointing it out. "And the people we're watching walk down the street probably look disappointed because their hair is absolutely ridiculous."

Jonas and Mateo took that in.

"To use vintage language that Jonas will appreciate," Mateo said, "I believe we've been 'schooled.'"

"Nice view? Ah, with ice cream!" my dad said. The three of us turned around and saw him standing awkwardly at the doorway to the roof. I quickly wondered and then ruled out whether I'd said anything I shouldn't have within earshot of my parents. "There's nothing like a view with dessert. That's what I always say. And Mateo!" Dad continued, giving him a hug, but oddly keeping his eyes on Jonas, "It's wonderful to see you."

Mateo smiled. "It's nice to see you too."

"And you I haven't met yet," Dad said, nodding at Jonas over Mateo's shoulders.

"My name is Jonas, sir. Thank you for having me over." Jonas extended his hand to shake my dad's.

Mateo looked at me over my dad's arm and mouthed, *Sir*? *Oooh*! I felt the heat crawl up my cheeks again and wondered why we hadn't invented anything yet to stop blushing.

"Why are you up here, Dad?" I asked, even though it was pretty clear he wanted to see who the new boy in our group was. He was embarrassing me.

"Oh! Um, well…maybe now's not the right time, but I wanted to share some good news."

"We want to hear good news," Mateo, Jonas, and I said in unison. My dad raised his eyebrows.

"Alrighty, well, your mom heard from her friend at the hospital about how Mrs. Stein continues to give gifts to society."

"She left a donation in her will?" I asked.

"Not exactly, not with money. Remember how she donated her brain to research? It looks like she, like her brain, boosted scientific understanding of something complicated I can't repeat. Had to do with cells in the part of the brain that has to do with resilience following trauma. I think the term she used was 'flashbulb' memory."

"Flashbulb?" I asked.

"Ah, yes, I forgot that I'm ancient and you wouldn't have heard that before."

"A flashbulb," Jonas chimed in, "was the flash of the original cameras. It was a light bulb. It became the name of a memory of things that are really emotional and kept by the brain instead of forgotten. Like, someone would remember where they were when they found out about, I don't know, an assassination, and maybe even that they were wearing their blue shirt when they heard the news. But they wouldn't remember much about that day if it had been a regular one."

"Impressive," my dad said earnestly. Mateo winked at me secretly. "Yes, so Mrs. Stein is boosting research on thriving in spite of trouble, or maybe even because of it, I'm not sure."

I thought back to my last conversation with her and the document she'd had framed—the missing person form her grandfather had filled out about the brother he'd lost in the Holocaust. "After I lost Nava," she'd said, "I was devastated and angry but looked at this document, framed on my shelf, and realized I had to continue living for the sake of my ancestors, so their acts of heroism wouldn't be for nothing and so those acts could continue through me." I wondered if she'd chosen that path and her actions had changed her brain, or if her brain had set her path for her.

"Well, anyway, I'll let you get back to your ice cream," my dad said. "Carry on!"

After the door closed behind him, the three of us were quiet in our individual thoughts and desserts for a few minutes. Jonas understood it first. Mateo got it second. I would have if I hadn't been thinking about my conversation with Mrs. Stein.

"Obie," Mateo said. "Did you hear what your dad said?"

"Yes . . .?"

Call Me Obie

"We have another item to add to the 'what we have' list."
Jonas paused. "Mrs. Stein's brain."

Chapter 17

I'd never knowingly hurt anyone or put them at risk. I'd even always avoided stepping on ant trails. For me to kill a bunch of harmless ants, the danger caused by not stepping on them would have to be high. Like, someone would have to threaten me by saying, "Obie, if you don't step on this ant trail, you'll be attacked by thieves. Or, a crazy Humanist couple will come after you, your parents, and your friends." Something like that. I mean, even when I was having angry fantasies about attacking Stella, I knew I would never actually do anything about it.

Back in Jonas' lab I was the one who pointed out that we couldn't actually "treat" Stella because she was already getting care at the hospital. Maybe the anti-swelling serum or the neural stem cell regeneration tonic Jonas told us about was working. It would be wrong to interfere. Really, what were we going to do, a brain transplant? Nut-so.

Then I received a message on my comm that made me forget to breathe.

122

"YOU AND YOUR LITTLE FRIEND SHOULD SAY YOUR PRAYERS BEFORE BED TONIGHT BECAUSE G0D HASN'T HEARD YOU YET. STELLA'S CONDITION REMAINS UNCHANGED." Below the words was a photo of my bedroom. My bedspread was floral blue and green, except for where Malloy's dark shadow lay. I could see his bulky silhouette clearly. His head actually reached my pillow and his legs appeared distended because of the angle of the light.

My fear made me hunch over as if I'd been punched in the stomach with an icy hand.

"Obie," Jonas said, "just go to the police. Tell them the situation but don't mention the spleen or Mateo. If they make the connection after talking to Stella's parents, we'll say you had no idea."

"But then you'll get in trouble," I said. "Big trouble. They'll uncover your entire lab."

Jonas touched his necklace. "I made choices. I did what I wanted to."

"Jonas," Mateo piped up. "I don't want Obie or her parents to get hurt either, but you could go to jail. You could lose all your freedom."

"Better me alone than the three of us," Jonas answered.

I'd never felt so low in my life. There was the paralyzing what-have-I-gotten-into, the all-the-ways-I-thought-people-might-hate-me-are-coming-true, and a good amount of now-what. All mixed together and churned in my stomach. Should I tell my parents? What would they think of me? I'd always been so good, and now I was mixed up with the black market for organ printing and getting death threats. I could never,

ever tell them I'd put all of us in danger. I pictured my dad's disappointed expression; I'd only seen it once or twice when he was lecturing about something or other and I'd cut him off, like, "Can't we talk about sports or anything normal?" He'd frowned and his blue eyes had darkened and looked really sad, and I'd felt as if I were choking on my tears. And my mom thought I could be a brain surgeon one day. She'd said so after Mrs. Stein's eye surgery. What would she think now about her little criminal?

Think. I commanded myself. *Think.* Things cannot be this bad. I cannot be forced to choose between my family and my friends' safety. And I cannot let everyone down. I made myself a mental worksheet:

Brief Mental Advice Board:
How would Dad say to solve this? I have no idea.
What would Mom say? I have no idea.
Mrs. Stein? Anyone else? No idea.
Just me.

"We are focusing on the police and ourselves instead of the main problem, which is Stella's injury," I said. The ideas were coming to me almost at the same time as I was saying them. "We only have one choice. Either we help Stella, or we don't. If we don't, since we just learned she isn't improving, this will end up badly for everyone—her and us. If we do, there's at least a chance she could recover, and all will be well. Her parents would probably leave us alone because their threats have always been tied to her condition."

"So, you're saying we don't really have anything to lose by helping?" Mateo asked.

"I'm saying that we have everything to lose and she has nothing to lose."

"That sounds like one dangerous combination," Jonas said. "How are we going to do this?"

Chapter 18

We started with the digital poster bright and early the next morning. The idea of a brain transplant (partial transplant, as Jonas kept pointing out) made my hands sweat. But what else could we do? There was a big hole in Stella's head that we at least needed to fill, and hopefully to fill with enough brain and medicine to make her function well enough to pass off to her parents. Jonas thought it might be possible for transplanted brain matter to connect with the brain that was already in there and for this whole thing to work. He explained it had to do with the tonic everything was soaking in—neural stem cells that could take any form would act as a bridge between the old and the new—but I missed most of what he said. We were going to mess with a brain. With two brains. Wow.

I didn't know if a brain transplant was what Malloy had in mind when he shared Stella's medical images with me, but those sure came in handy when we needed to figure out which part of Mrs. Stein's head we needed. Jonas was placed in charge of getting the medical scans onto our comms in a format where we'd be able to share and upload them to any other equipment. Mateo and I were in charge of figuring out where the brain was probably being stored and how we'd get it. Planning what we'd do with it when we found it, we all decided we'd tackle that together last.

The good news was that scientific research on organs was done at the basement level of the hospital building where Stella was kept. It was the same building where Mateo had undergone his transplant. That meant if we could get the brain, we wouldn't have to transport it very far.

But how would we get into the basement? There had to be security set up. We wondered if we could use the EmpathSpin App to enter through another person, but no hospital employees we could find seemed to be on it—that was probably against their rules. That's where Mateo came up with a good idea. He'd ask to tour the basement as a student and a recent spleen recipient. He called it a "reconnaissance mission." Jonas hooked him up with a retinal camera that Mateo wore over his blue eye. Altogether, you couldn't really see the camera, it just made Mateo's blue shimmer a bit less. "From now on," Mateo announced, looking at himself in the mirror, "we don't call anything a silver lining but a blue one."

"What if he can't get in?" I asked Jonas as we watched the hospital enter Mateo's line of sight via our video feed. We could see his longitude and latitude listed in the lower right corner of the screen.

"He'll get in," Jonas answered. "He's too cute and sad not to."

Mateo approached the check-in console and a man's face appeared before us.

"Welcome to our facility. How may I help you?"

"Um, my name is Mateo and I . . ."

I leaned forward. I'd never heard Mateo use that voice before. Usually, he spoke so fast I needed him to slow down.

"Is he freaking out?" Jonas said.

"Nah, he's acting," I reassured him.

Mateo continued, "I was treated here recently because I got shot during a beach clean-up. One minute I was picking up a lost toy doll, the kind where the eyes can open and close on their own, and the next I woke up here. My mother was crying. She said I'd lost my spleen."

"Nice," I said. Jonas nodded.

"I guess I just wanted to say thanks to the staff who treated me, especially the lab scientists who are working so diligently to keep medicine at the forefront of innovation. May I meet them to say so in person?"

I burst out laughing. Those were the words from the commercial Mateo, and I used to act out. I think it was for a drug that promised to prevent split hair ends but all I can really remember is that for weeks after seeing it Mateo would make me walk in front of him and say, "I'm working diligently to keep you at the forefront of innovation, Obie."

"Hang on," the man said. His face disappeared for a moment and then returned. "May I scan you for pathogens and elevated temperature?"

"Sure." Mateo stood still as a light ran down his face and body.

"Okay, you are clear," the man continued. "Go to the elevators and someone will meet you."

When Mateo reached the shiny doors, he winked at his reflection.

"Was that for us?" I asked.

"Yep. Your friend is quite the charmer."

"That's why I keep him around."

The doors opened and an old man stepped forward. The closer he came to the camera, the older I realized he was. His hands were skin on bones with thick, blue veins running up them, but still they maintained grace. His neck skin sagged. His brown eyes were buried beneath wrinkled lids but felt familiar somehow. When he opened his toothless mouth to greet Mateo, I realized why.

"He was at Mrs. Stein's funeral," I said. "That's weird, I wonder how they knew each other."

"Wewcome, thun," he said, reaching out for Mateo's hand. Mateo must have looked confused because the man followed up with, "Ah, excuthe me," and reached into his pocket. He brought out a set of teeth. I had to lean forward to get a closer look. I'd never seen anything like that before.

"They're called dentures," Jonas informed me. "I think they went out of style in 2035."

"Getting vintage retail ideas?" I asked.

"You bet."

Once the man inserted the teeth into his mouth, he tried again. "Welcome, son. And sorry about that; I take them off

129

when I'm working because they bug me. I'm more of a fruit smoothie guy anyway, so doesn't matter."

Bravo to Mateo for not laughing. "I'm more of a rip-meat-apart-with-your-teeth kind of guy," he answered. Jonas and I chuckled.

"Please, come with me. I am sorry for what happened to you. I'd love to show you where I work," the man said. "My name is Penn, by the way."

The elevator ride went down to the basement and the doors opened before the entry to a rather boring laboratory. The walls were beige aside from one screen showing some kind of list, maybe an organ inventory. There were countertops with jars and vials, really fancy-looking microscopes, a few older generation printers, and lots of refrigerators. Penn showed Mateo some pretty cool images of cells from different parts of the body. The cardiac cells looked very tough to me. "Can you ask him if heart cells are stronger than others?" I typed to Mateo so it would appear on his side of the retinal camera he was wearing.

"Would you say the cells in the heart are sturdier than others?" Mateo asked.

"Cardiac cells have contractile proteins. They also differentiate earlier on relative to other cells in the developing fetus to enable blood to be pumped around the body," Penn said.

I took that to mean yes. To use a cliché, my strong heart cells swelled with pride. I bet that mine were even stronger than most because of my treatment.

"May I see some of the tools you use to study the organs?" Mateo requested.

Penn led him over to a device I knew from before—a surgical robot. This one was smaller than the one I'd used at Mrs. Stein's home. It looked like a four-legged spider, but instead of the belly there was a cabinet with interchangeable parts that would probably go onto the spider's hands. The operator console was separate and lay on a nearby countertop. It had a physical keyboard and a two-handed remote control. Next to it was a small platform.

"The organ would go here," Penn said, gesturing to it.

"Like a brain?"

"Yes, within a vial of cerebrospinal fluid, a brain would go here."

Jonas leaned forward and started typing out the list of questions we'd thought up.

"How do you know which slice of the brain you are taking when you dissect the brain?"

"Well," Penn said, pausing to press his index finger against the front of his dentures, "we don't take slices as much as specific areas. They don't need to be a slice, and usually they aren't since brain function is less organized like sliced bread and more like a . . . bean casserole where the beans haven't been mixed well because you want all the scoops you serve to be a little different." He looked at Mateo and gave him a wrinkled smile. I heard Mateo chuckle. We were all starting to like this guy. "So, anyway, we use electric stimulation and an atlas of the brain parts to understand the layout of that particular person's brain."

"What's a brain atlas?"

"It's like a general brain map that we personalize to the individual patient since everyone's brains are a little different. I mean, all humans will have their specific casserole scoops about the same distance apart, like the part responsible for heartbeat and breathing is a certain shape and length away from the part that helps code experience into long-term memory, but there's a little variation between people and we want to be precise. Also, some of the functions are not clearly lumped into one area."

"Like what?"

"Well, I mentioned the part that helps code memory. Memory function isn't that, excuse the pun, cut and dry. It's complicated . . . there's the stuff we remember forever, like our wedding day, and then there's stuff we forget right away, like what the inside of the elevator you rode down just now looked like. And all that is handled differently."

"So where is memory stored?" That wasn't on the script we were sending Mateo. I thought he was getting genuinely interested in the whole brain science thing.

"I wish we knew! I could tell you which part of the brain has responsibility for which task, but is memory held in the cells in those parts and how so? We still don't know exactly," Penn answered.

Mateo, Jonas, and I were silent, pondering this. Then Jonas said, "We're getting off track," and typed in the next question.

"So, how would you get the robot to take out a specific piece of the brain?"

"That part is simple—I just tell it to. By the time I get to the robot, I already know the specific shape I'm interested in cutting out for analysis. The atlas tells me approximately where it is. The robot runs the electric stimulation to individualize the cut we were making."

"Electric stimulation?"

"Yes, the robot will send electric pulses at that part of the brain to see how the different cells respond and narrow down the target region. Here's an interesting thing—the way the electricity bounces off the cells depends on what those cells do. Like, the brain cells in areas that help us walk will reflect different colors than the ones in the area that helps us remember where we are or understand a pattern. And the older the patient, the more strongly those colors will appear because the cells are so differentiated."

"What does differentiated mean?"

"Ah, of course; it means distinguishable, like you can tell them apart. Scientists used to insert fluorescent proteins into brain cells in order to see them, but once we all started to live longer, scientists realized that these cells actually had visibly different properties under electrical stimulation. So, if you electrocuted my old brain, some parts would look yellow, some white, and maybe some green."

"So, the casserole is now an omelet with green onion sprinkled on top?"

"No, more like eggs cooked sunny side with green onion."

Mateo didn't skip a beat. "So, the robot helps you tell apart the different brain areas and then you can cut the right

133

one out. It follows the guidelines of the atlas and the electric output."

"Yes, precisely," Penn paused, then smiled again, "pun intended."

Jonas snorted.

"I don't think we even need the electrical output," I said. "Right? I mean, we're going to act off the brain imaging Malloy left in my room. We don't have the missing brain tissue that Stella lost in her fall."

"True," Jonas said, "but it's good to know what to expect from the robot."

"And these are where the organs are stored?" Mateo gestured to the refrigerators. This was our last and most important question. If we couldn't find Mrs. Stein's brain, and had no guarantee there was any other available, we'd have to put jelly into Stella's head and call it a day.

"Yes," Penn said. Mateo walked slowly over to the storage units. It sounded like Penn followed behind him.

"I don't see any type of locks, do you?" I asked Jonas.

"No . . . let me ask Mateo to turn his head a bit," he responded, typing into the system. A moment later, Mateo looked both left and right.

"Most in my profession organize by type but I also do so by age," Penn was still talking.

"Do they not protect the donated organs?" I wondered. "Maybe they're not as valuable as the tissues used for printing?"

"Hmmm," Jonas touched his necklace. "Let me ask Mateo to look at the doorway."

134

Mateo pivoted and looked back at where they entered. I spotted a scanner sticking out of the wall on the other side of the doorway.

"It's a single sign-on device," Jonas explained. "Penn must use it to enter the room and get access to everything inside."

"I don't remember him scanning his retina when they came in."

"Maybe Mateo wasn't looking in that direction?"

"Okay, Mateo, we're all set," Jonas wrote. "Excellent reconnaissance."

When Mateo thanked Penn for his time, Penn told him how happy he was to mentor the next generation. I felt some guilt settle in my stomach but told myself that we weren't totally lying to the man, we were truly interested in this science. In fact, we intended to apply what we'd learned very soon.

Chapter 19

I tried to not get dirt or leaves on the vintage suit from Jonas' store as I waited. I was crouching in the bushes in the parking lot, anticipating the moment when the chemicals dancing around the pollution filters would hit icy particles around the air filter. Then they'd make a brief but thick ice fog right in front of the security cameras, just like they did above my building. It seemed that hospital employees were usually dropped off by a corporate shuttle and I didn't want to be seen as a lone wolf just walking on in.

My thighs were starting to ache from squatting and my shoulder pads were driving me crazy. I was covered in sweat because I was scared and because the old clothing I was wearing had no ventilation. This was definitely one of those *How did I get here?* moments.

"So how are we going to handle security?" Mateo had asked earlier while putting drops into his blue eye because the camera had dried it out.

"How are we going to do an illegal partial brain transplant?" I retorted. Now that Mateo's "reconnaissance" mission was over, we had to turn to the next problem.

"The good news," Jonas answered, looking up at me from disinfecting the equipment, "is that her brain injury has saved us a lot of work. Her head is already open, and patients with her problem usually have a removable casing over their skull so that the treatment can take place."

"Oh, phew," I said and wiped my hand across my forehead.

"Ease up on the sarcasm," Mateo told me, "and start prepping for the procedure."

"Me?"

"Yes," Jonas said. "From what Mateo has shared, you are quite the eye surgeon."

I remembered the robot-assisted mock eye surgery I'd done at Mrs. Stein's home before the shooting—before everything. It seemed like it was a thousand years ago.

Mateo continued, "You have the most experience between the three of us, and Jonas downloaded as much of the instructional software for brain dissection as he could find anonymously, so get cracking Obie, MD."

After that, I'd gotten to practice snipping at fake brain samples using Jonas' organ handling equipment and an old kidney he'd printed for practice years ago. He drew some lines and bumps onto it with a marker to make it more brain-like and then stood behind me, guiding my arms as I held the tools that steered the surgical pens as we listened to the instructions. Since human brain transplants were illegal, we planned to use the guidelines for transplants in animals which we'd found in some ancient medical textbook. How could a robot know what it was holding anyway?

The trickiest part was holding the piece of kidney-brain in the right way so we could reinsert it into the space we'd just cut it out of. Then, a thin material called a fusogen sheet would not only hold the implanted part in place, but help it reconnect with the receiving brain. I'd say, by the end of our rehearsal, I was 85% confident we could do this as a team that relied almost entirely on a surgical robot, and 15% lost in Jonas' scent. It reminded me of trees and hiking paths after a rainy day.

We'd planned to launch our operation (pun intended, as Penn would say) early in the morning.

My confidence level went down to about 5% as I waited in the bushes. It was so hard to calm down, I turned the biofeedback monitor off my comm so House wouldn't pipe up with some deep breathing recommendation. I'd wanted more time to train, but Malloy had been messaging me pretty consistently from a temporary account named "Yollam," which was Malloy spelled backwards, and as Mateo pointed out, lame and uncreative enough to be real. I guessed that Stella's condition wasn't improving, or maybe was getting worse, and he was just sitting next to her hating me. When he wrote, "THE HEALING WINDOW IS CLOSING AND WE'RE ABOUT TO OPEN THE ONE IN YOUR ROOM AND CRAWL IN" we decided to reply to make him stall.

"THE FOREFRONT OF INNOVATION IS ABOUT TO REACH STELLA. WAIT." Mateo came up with it; he said it was sufficiently vague to buy us some time. Malloy didn't reply, which we took as a good sign.

When the fog appeared, I stood, brushed myself off quickly, made sure no one was nearby, and approached the building. I'd left my tablet at home since it was the student kind, and Jonas had given me a device called a "clip board" to carry, saying no one would notice it wasn't digital if I carried myself with authority. So, I threw my shoulders back, pulled strands of my hair out of my mouth and tucked them into my blonde wig, and marched right in to meet my fate.

A security guard actually looked up at me and nodded as I waited for the elevator. Jonas spoke into my ear bud. He'd figured out how to build one out of his immersive videogame equipment. I thought he sounded defensive for not doing it earlier for Mateo. He kept saying that these days people weren't used to thinking for themselves because they expected machines to do it for them. He also sounded kind of like my dad right then. Gross.

I felt my heart quicken on the ride down to the basement. It beat so fast that I reminded myself how cardiac cells were really strong, and I was very unlikely to have a heart attack, even when the clip board slipped out of my sweaty hands and clattered to the floor. When the doors opened, I was wiping my palms on my pants and picking it up frantically. "Obie, remember that the robot will do most of the work, okay?" Mateo said. I nodded. The door to Penn's lab was closed and the security scanner stood a few feet in front of me.

During our planning we hadn't been certain about how I would get into the lab. Mateo had a few snapshots of Penn's eyes but nothing close to a retinal scan. Jonas said it was worth just trying them out anyway because the scanner at Penn's lab's entryway wasn't a device he had recognized, so it was probably really old and unsophisticated.

I held the images we had of Penn's eyes in front of the scanner and waved them around a bit. Nothing happened.

"Hey, can you look at the right side?" Jonas said.

I did so, and then saw words I'd never seen strung together into a sentence before.

CARDIAC IDENTIFICATION SYSTEM.

Eh?

"Remember when I said the security scanner looked old-fashioned?" Jonas asked.

I nodded, unable to speak.

"I would like to retract that statement. It's actually cutting-edge tech based on the electrical signal of a heart."

Mateo uttered a big cuss word in Spanish. I won't repeat it.

"No wonder Penn just had one security lock. It's like this is the big one, and I bet the others open when they're in close proximity to this one, or to the user," Jonas said.

I muttered, "Tell me more! Now is a great time to hear the theory of security technology." Then I realized they could hear me because my ear bud was translating vibrations from my jaw into a normal volume for them. "I think we may need to call this off," I said. I hoped my eye cam wouldn't wash out from the tears pooling in my eyes. To have planned so much. To have come this far. To have worn shoulder pads. How could I just turn back? I put my hands on top of the scanner and leaned forward, resting my head on my arms.

BEEP. ALL CLEAR.

The lab door unlocked and slid open.

What? I thought just as I heard the word in my earpiece, making me think for a moment the tech had figured out how to read my thoughts—until I realized my team had said it at the same time.

"Your heart is a match somehow," Jonas said. I mentally assigned him an award for Most Obvious Statement during the mission we were running.

"Don't ask why, just go in before it changes its mind," Mateo urged me.

I ran in and the door closed behind me. I was in the lab, and it was because of my heart—my formerly defective heart—which had been a source of blood, oxygen, and stress since my early life. Now it was a critical solution in my time of need.

Chapter 20

Mrs. Stein's brain was in a jar in the refrigerator marked "S – 100+." It looked like an oversized gray raisin. What made my stomach flip around, though, was that I was holding part of my friend and mentor. This organ had been behind the eyes that had looked at me, the mouth that had spoken to me, the hands that had baked rugelach, and the mind that had known me. I missed her so much it choked me.

I had to wash my hands five times until the system said I was clean enough and allowed me to put on gloves and pick up the jar. It was lighter than I expected, lighter than the weight of how burdened I suddenly felt, lighter than everything I knew made up a human being. I carefully placed it on the platform by the dissection robot and stepped back. Jonas and Mateo wisely remained silent, maybe not to distract me, or maybe because they didn't know what to say.

I didn't have time to waste, though. It was early, but who could know if Penn would suddenly show up, inspired to begin his workday ahead of normal hours? I closed my eyes and gave myself one second to feel nervous, only one, before I took a deep breath and opened them to begin. I'd called our plan AIDE—Assess, Import, Dissect, and Enter. I'd make the robot measure the brain and locate all the important parts we'd need, then I'd put the images of the slices we wanted into the computer system, and then I'd pull those slices out of the brain. Enter was probably the wrong word for using a neural stem cell protocol to insert the part we'd taken out into Stella's brain, but no one had been able to come up with anything better.

Mrs. Stein's brain already had a few cuts here and there, which I'd anticipated since my dad had said she was already contributing to research, but it seemed like the area in the frontal lobe we wanted was intact. I tapped the kiosk screen to fully wake up the robot, then put on the goggles and slipped my hands into the surgical gloves. On one part of the screen, I could see the brain. On the other, a menu of options.

"Start the procedure," I said after picking the dissection protocol I wanted. The floor vibrated a bit with sudden robotic activity. Metal clamps emerged from the brain stand and held the jar in place. The words "Stereotax initiated" appeared in my view as a metal archway slid around the jar. It buzzed as white lights shot out and formed a grid across the organ. I stared, open-mouthed, as the machine measured Mrs. Stein's brain and began assessing exactly where each part of it was. When "Stage One" was complete, the lighting changed, and the lines became very thin and specific. "Electric Mapping Initiated" flashed before me and a bright array scanned one area of the brain at a time, starting at the bottom—the stem—

then moving up and spreading to all sides. In response, the brain tissue reflected colors. I watched it all from the robot kiosk.

First, there was this blushing atmosphere of different soft pockets of color. Some were yellow, speckled with turquoise, others deep blue with purple streaks that reminded me of a sunset. It was like watching a beautifully arranged flower bouquet grow out of one stalk. I was mesmerized; I'd expected to be disgusted today, not shown moving art that literally reflected the diversity within one of our most important organs. What was the purpose of these regions and cells and molecules and atoms? Were they born to deliver blue, or did we get to decide how our internal selves would be painted and work?

I slipped off the goggles and stepped up to the jar, leaning forward and looking at the glass curvature. Bright green was spreading sideways, seeping slowly like the way a bubble will show the stripes of a rainbow in a zig-zagging pattern, one color edging out the rest as it bends over the side. How could I have spent my life so focused on my imperfect heart when I had this beauty inside of me? How could I have ever cared so much about what others thought when I was made from parts with such gorgeous purpose?

I walked around the vessel and looked at it again, this time seeing the glass closest to the frontal lobe, where we'd be dissecting. The reflection of the purple on the glass was complicated by many small sections that moved individually. I looked closely; they looked like little purple people. It reminded me of a toy I'd had as a kid where I could arrange small TV blocks however I wanted and a little electronic person would look like he was walking from one into the other. As I gazed at the pattern, a larger figure emerged that reminded me of a baby. Then it became more slender, like a little girl. Its movement changed from a waddle to elegant steps as it grew hair that blew in the wind.

"Do you guys see that?" I asked.

"The colors? Yes, pretty bod," Mateo answered.

"You're probably getting a better show than us, Obie," Jonas added. "The retinal cam strips out some layers."

I didn't press them for more but checked my biofeedback on my comm to make sure I wasn't having a nervous breakdown or something. The human figure on the glass was running, then dancing, then soaring. Then it turned into one large purple blob. I held my face as close to the jar as I could without wiping my nose on it. And suddenly the blob became a face. It was shaped like an oval with shadows that became facial structure—cheekbones, a chin, a small nose, and closed eyes. I stopped breathing and my skin prickled. I was looking at the face of a young child; it was even the same size. And then the eyes opened and stared blindly in my direction.

I screamed and jumped back.

"What is it? Obie? Are you okay?" The words came jumbled through my earpiece.

"I, um . . . it . . ." I placed my hand on my chest and tried to breathe, then sat down and put my head between my knees. "I saw something. Saw something."

"Where?"

"There." I looked up and pointed, but the colors were gone and the lights off.

"Electric Mapping Complete" was scrawled across the kiosk screen.

"Obie, *amiga*, you need to calm down," Mateo said. "Breathe in so your chest rises and let it out slowly."

I tried to breathe in and couldn't.

"Obie, try again. I've done this every morning since the shooting. Trust me."

My poor friend. My poor, poor friend. The idea of what Mateo had suffered, and continued to suffer, snapped me back to the present. I breathed deeply three times, then wiped my cheeks and stood. "I feel better," I said, although my back was cold from my sweat.

The kiosk flashed a message:

UPLOAD RESECTION SPECIFICATIONS . . .
UPLOAD RESECTION SPECIFICATIONS . . .
UPLOAD RESECTION SPECIFICATIONS . . .

"Obie, it wants you to import the image we made from Stella's digital poster, so it knows what piece to cut out of Mrs. Stein's brain," Jonas said.

"Oh! Right." I opened the image on my comm and swiped it over to the kiosk, got an unused flask from Penn's storage unit, and put the goggles on again. The image showed Stella's brain with an inset, like a map legend, of the missing piece. As it rotated before me, scrolling text told me that "VR Stereotax" was underway, which I thought meant the machine was checking out the missing piece. It gave me the output of:

146

EST. MAJORITY OVERLAP MEDIAL PREFRONTAL CORTEX = 85.79%

EST. TISSUE IMPACT DIFFUSED WITHIN FRONTAL CORTEX

"I'm glad the system understood the poster image," Jonas said, approvingly. I heard a noise that sounded like a high five. Dorks. It was time for D—dissect—not for congratulating ourselves.

I put on the gloves, picked up the controllers, and directed the robotic arms to open the toolbox in its center and equip its "hands" with tools. I could feel the moment where my gloves woke up. They guided my hands to move the tools into position above the correct region of the brain. Then the robot and I went to work.

I admit my stomach turned over a few times as I inserted the first cutting instrument into the organ. But viewing it all over video made the experience far less nauseating than I think it would have been if I'd been looking right at Mrs. Stein's brain. And overall, it was less scary than seeing a purple child give me a zombie look in the reflection of a glass jar. So perhaps that terrifying moment was the best surgical prep I could have asked for. See? Mom always taught me to look for silver linings.

The tissue was squishy; I could feel the consistency since the robot was giving me haptic feedback—a feature I chose not to turn off, so I'd know if I were about to poke a hole through the entire organ. As I wheeled a thin, fibrous applicator around the area I wanted, the resistance I felt changed to easier and then hard. Jonas and Mateo had agreed not to talk to me unless it was absolutely necessary, so I wondered if Mateo was thinking of the same old cartoon—one where the cowboy lassoed the cow only to be pulled off his own horse and dragged through the dirt.

The robot checked the placement of my lasso and, satisfied that it matched the missing piece of Stella's brain, initiated laser heat to cut the connective tissue. Since this brain's donor was already dead, the system didn't need to worry much about collateral damage.

Did I just think of Mrs. Stein as an anonymous brain donor? I brushed the idea away. Time to focus.

I pulled a gray and pink lump out of the brain and laid it on the platform. Then I changed to fine-cutting mode and began to apply low-power laser beams to the lump to make the shape more closely match our requirements. Small amounts of smoke rose up and I was grateful I couldn't smell through the goggles' nose piece. Following the guidelines, I could see overlaid by my goggles, I pulled excess tissue out of the way with tweezers as I burned off the rest. I directed the robot to put what was left, that precious little puzzle piece, into the jar and to fill it with the cerebrospinal tonic that would keep it ready for phase two: Stella.

So, we'd done AID—Assess, Import, and Dissect.

"Obie, that was amazing," Jonas said.

"Truly," Mateo added.

"Thank you." I allowed myself a congratulatory moment. It was the best way to ignore what was coming next. Enter.

Chapter 21

I had to wheel the robot into Stella's room since I didn't know if there'd be another one there. It was the weirdest walk I'd ever gone on. My hands had just removed a chunk of brain matter and plopped it into a jar, and now here they were pushing this cart into the elevator and down a hallway. There were more employees milling around and I placed my "clipboard" on top of the sheet covering the robot so I'd look official again. *Dum dee dum dee dum, don't mind me!* But, as I passed through doorways, I heard soft beeping noises and realized that it was the sound of security features unlocking — the same sound as when I'd gotten access to enter the basement lab. My heart was opening doors again. No wonder no one was questioning me. I paused and slipped the clipboard under the sheet. Sorry, Jonas, but with all due respect to the 2020s, that prop isn't going to get me any new fans today.

I slowed down when I reached the waiting room where Jonas and I had encountered Stella's mom. It was a small ward, but I needed to figure out which room was Stella's as quickly as possible. So, here's where I took slight advantage of my powerful heart. I just opened the door to different patient rooms a teensy bit and looked in. I guess you could say I was feeling a new sensation some people would call confident, buoyant, or maybe even high. Let's look behind door number one!

I peeked in on an older woman in a reclining chair. She had bandages over her eyes, but when I opened the door, she turned her head in my direction so I closed it quietly and moved on to door number two. I shut that one pretty quickly after spotting a sleeping man whose legs ended slightly below the knees. I felt myself start to come back to earth. Perhaps this is not a game show after all.

The room at the end of the hall had a symbol pasted around the top middle of the door. It looked like an old-fashioned anti-smoking symbol but instead of crossing out a cigarette it went over a heart.

"Does that mean it doesn't use the cardiac identification system to let people into the room?" I whispered.

"Either that or it means 'no organ' applies to whoever is in the room," Mateo said. "Like, so the nurses respect the patient and their Humanist beliefs."

I slid the door open. It was hard to recognize her at first, but Stella lay upright in bed, her eyes closed, her chest moving slowly with each breath, and her shaved head covered in casing with one slim tube emerging from the center.

I wheeled the robot in and closed the door behind me.

It's hard to explain, even though I was conscious of it, but I didn't see Stella. I mean, I certainly looked at her, but in a detached way. It was as if I could feel the humanity in me, the part that made me recognize everyone as a person, slide back from the tips of my fingers into my palms, up my arms, and then across the rest of me. She became a body, the head had a hole in it that I was going to fill, and nothing more was going on. I think that's how it had to be. I think that, otherwise, I would have cried.

The casing had been sewn to the scalp with plastic sutures that I directed the robot to snip off. I didn't look when it pulled the cover off. I had a view of the cavity in my goggles that made the experience like watching an interactive movie. I directed a neuronavigational wand into the center of the hole in Stella's head so the robot could assess the surrounding tissue before the transplant. The tool gave a few reassuring beeps to tell me it was working, evaluating the walls around it, like a wall climber judging the surface of a cave. Then it stopped. I selected "exit" from the menu of options, and it didn't respond. Strange.

I gave the wand a gentle virtual pull outward by pantomiming in the air with my gloves and it still didn't move, the robotic arms held it right in place. Stranger.

"Guys?" I whispered. "Can you hear me?"

"Affirmative," Mateo said into my ear. "But no idea why it froze. Jonas is looking for—"

And then the line disconnected.

"Hello? Guys?" I whispered. *What, am I trying not to wake up Stella?* "HELLO?" I yelled. No answer. I should have treasured that moment of silence before what happened next.

I never knew that robots could scream like people.

WEE-OOO-WEE-OOO-WEE-OOO-WEE-OOO-WEE-OOO-WEE-OOO

I ripped the goggles off my face, covered my ears, and staggered over to the kiosk to see the screen.

HUMAN BRAIN TISSUE DETECTED

ILLEGAL PROCEDURE BLOCKED

HALT—INVASIVE PROCESS

HALT—ALL AMBIENT COMMUNICATION SYSTEMS

HALT—

Remember how my dad always said not to over-rely on technology—to use your brain, not look everything up, and so on? Maybe that's what led me to throw a stool against the kiosk. Well, to slam it against the surface over and over until the surface cracked and then broke open. The robotic screaming stopped, and I dropped the stool and tried to open the door, but it was locked. I collapsed against the wall, sliding down to a squat, and resting my head against my crossed forearms.

I think that if my heart hadn't been 3D printed, it would have exploded from fear and nerves. I'd been left, cut off from the outside world, in a room with a frozen robot and a body with a hole in its brain. Security was probably coming down the hall to get me. I bet I had five to ten minutes before I was hauled off, and for what? A brain dissection without a transplant. Now Stella's parents wouldn't have to come after my family; we'd all be in trouble anyway, and Stella would stay how she was.

No. With the one-word thought I stood up and surveyed the room. I could not, would not, leave it like this. Stopping now would mean that the Humanists had won even though we'd fought back, and that would mean that I was defenseless. Not in the same way as Mateo and the volunteers cleaning the beach, but still. I refused to live in a world where that was true. I had to do something, to take action.

What do I have that I can use?

I approached the toolbox at the center of the robot and opened it.

I have everything.

Chapter 22

The fusogen sheet nearly ripped when I pulled it out. *Dang it.* It was as light as an ironed sheet of facial tissue, and I needed it to be the right size and shape to hold the piece of Mrs. Stein's brain and fit it into Stella's head.

I pulled the images of Stella's brain scan from Malloy's poster onto my comm and then projected them two-dimensionally onto the wall at actual size. Then I picked up a scalpel that looked like a right triangle and gently held the fusogen paper up to the wall. *Breathe.* The paper fluttered with my exhale. *Okay, don't breathe.* At first, I pressed too hard, and the scalpel actually cut into the wall. Then, I lightly cut the outline of Stella's missing part out of the paper and put that precious puzzle piece onto the tray.

No time to admire my work. I heard footsteps in the hall, and they must have been loud ones in order to be audible in this tiny, insulated room. I pressed small, circular stickers labeled "micro-connector tabs" onto the paper—as many as I could fit across the small surface. Then I laid the piece of Mrs.

Stein's brain on top. It lined up with the borders it touched pretty well.

More noise outside the door, and now I could hear muffled voices. I rolled the fusogen paper around the brain piece, and I admit, smiled as I knew what Mateo would say right then: It's like wrapping a small burrito, *amiga*. Just like that.

More like a flower bouquet wrapped in paper, I'd have answered. Like, the tiniest gray and pink cone of mushy, gushy flowers you've ever seen.

Lightly holding Mrs. Stein's brain wrapped in the paper, I approached Stella's head. One try. Get it right the first time. I slipped it in, slowly allowing the paper to slide past my gloved fingers bit by bit. I held it in place with one hand by the edge of the paper. As the growth serum inside Stella's head soaked through the paper, the micro-connector tabs expanded and poked out of either side of the paper. They looked like the thumb tacks Jonas used to pin up clothing in his store, but much shorter and smaller. When I cautiously let go, the implant held in place.

At this point I could hear drilling noise on the other side of the door. *But I'm not done*, I thought. *Not yet*.

I quickly put the casing back over Stella's skull and re-stitched the loops I'd cut off earlier. Then I bowed my head. "Please," I murmured, "please heal. Please let this heal. Thank you."

That was it. That was how I performed an illegal brain transplant. All that was left was waiting for my arrest. I went to the window and looked out at the garden. We were on ground level and I could admire the pink and orange flowers. I was surprised by my blonde-headed reflection and remembered I was wearing a disguise. If Stella recovered, I would donate my wig to her.

A hummingbird whizzed past the window, hungry for a meal. I wondered if I'd get a window in prison, or if maybe they'd give me house arrest because of my age. I glanced up, hoping to see as much of the sky as the surrounding buildings would allow, to take it in while I could.

At the top of the pane there was a transparent label: CONTACT SECURITY PERSONNEL TO OPEN WINDOW.

I supposed that made sense. They didn't want people climbing in from the outside. Jonas, Mateo, and I had hoped I might be able to get in that way but decided the idea was unlikely.

We'd made such a great team. I hoped to see them again one day.

Now the drilling stopped, and the door started beeping electronically. The voices came through more clearly.

"How did . . .?"

"Almost in!"

And finally, "Stand back. . ."

I looked back at the sky for my last time. What would I tell my parents? The truth. That's all that I could do. And apologize.

A familiar box labeled CARDIAC IDENTIFICATION SYSTEM was affixed to the wall just above the window and on the outside. The same kind that had been outside Penn's lab. I wondered if it had shut down the same way the one by the door had locked on me, or if I could just . . .

When I opened the window, the hummingbird flew past me again. Maybe it even gave me a surprised look, but by then I was looking down at the windowsill, one of my legs thrown over it, the surface of the wall scraping my shin through my pants. I brought my other leg over carefully, not wanting to ruin this opportunity by falling, then slid down slowly until I was forced to let go. I felt a mild shock in my ankles when I hit the ground, but I had no time to waste. I began to run, my 3D-printed heart beating with exertion and glee.

Chapter 23

"Obie?" my mom asked. "Everything okay? You've been very quiet this week." I stopped staring into space and focused on her face. "Hi, Obie!" she said, waving her hand in front of me. I looked down at the dinner plate she'd laid before me, then smiled. Burrito night.

After leaving the hospital, I'd waited until evening to turn on the Find Me function of my comm. Minutes later, Jonas and Mateo pulled up in a tan colored van that had a sliding door with a darker brown horizontal line running down the side. I only mention that because it actually made me pause—*Eh? What year is it?*—before Mateo yelled, "Get in!" Jonas drove as I filled them in.

"Honey," my dad started, snapping me back. "We know you've been experiencing a lot lately—the shooting and Mateo, switching to online classes for now, Mrs. Stein, then the news about Stella's fall. We thought we could talk about it."

I gazed at him. Jonas, Mateo, and I had decided the only thing to do was wait. Wait to hear news of Stella, wait until her dad threatened us again, wait until life felt like a new normal (abnormal?). The past week had felt like walking through gelatin. I answered my teachers when they called on me, I marked my answers on my homework assignments, I moved my body when it was PE. But what had happened, and not knowing what was going to happen, weighed on my soul every minute of the day. That and wondering if the wig had been enough to disguise me. If the wand could detect human brain tissue, what could have sensed me in the hospital that I didn't know about?

"How are you feeling?" my mom asked, putting her hand on mine.

"I feel dazed," I answered, honestly. "I don't know what to say."

"I've always favored actions over talk anyway," my dad offered. He had black beans stuck to the sides of his mouth, but I think my mom laughed because my dad is more of a talker than a doer.

"If I took action . . . what . . ." I stammered. "How would I know it was the right one?"

"Interesting question!" My dad laid his burrito down on the plate. My mom sighed.

"You could ask yourself if it felt right. Just to start," he continued, oblivious.

I thought about it. Did it feel right to put part of someone else's body into Stella's? It felt weird . . . but it didn't feel wrong. Not like stealing money would, or cheating.

"The issue with the internal judge, though," my dad said, "is that it's subjective. For example, taking the cookie from your friend's lunch box could feel justified because they owe you money. But should you take the cookie without asking? I say no."

Try taking someone's brain after they donated it to science, Dad. I wish I were worried about taking a cookie now.

"Another question: did you act respectfully? Did you do right by other people and yourself? If you'd asked for the cookie before taking it, I'd say so."

I didn't feel I'd acted disrespectfully. I mean, Mrs. Stein had donated her brain, and now that she was dead, I couldn't have asked her anyway. And I'd been trying to save Stella, not hurt her. I felt my stomach untwist a little.

"Last thing, what would an outside authority say?"

My stomach twisted right back up. I'd broken the law. But, in my defense, I'd been forced to. Right? It wasn't that I didn't feel responsible for my actions, but her dad was going to hurt me and my family and friends. It wasn't as if I'd just woken up one day and decided to break into a hospital and do brain surgery.

House gave me a massage in bed that night and I fell into a deep sleep as my pillow stroked my scalp and my mattress rubbed my shoulders. I dreamed that I was swimming in the middle of an ocean full of enormous waves. Every time one approached me, I ducked down into the water to swim beneath it instead of being swept up and tossed around. The waves came at me so fast that I barely had time to breathe in between. I realized I was sheltering a baby against my chest—a baby boy with one blue eye and one dark brown—and I hoped he could hold his breath as we went under again and again. Then I looked down and realized he was gone, and my arms were crossed against my torso, the scar from my childhood surgery visible on my chest. I heard my heartbeat loudly in my ears. It sounded like it was buzzing electronically. When I woke up, gasping, my comm was vibrating against my table with an urgent message from Mateo.

SHE WOKE UP.

"What do you mean he figured it out?"

We were standing in Jonas' lab and Mateo was sitting on the floor, fingering the lower rim of a burgundy crop top hanging off the back of a chair.

"I don't know, Obie," he said, looking up at me. "For the hundredth time, I got a message from Penn asking me to meet and to bring, I quote, 'your blonde-wigged friend.' He wrote that no one would get into trouble, he just wanted to talk. When I responded that I didn't know what he was talking about, he wrote that Stella was awake, and he had information for me."

Jonas inhaled audibly and placed his palms on top of his head. I tried to ignore the way his sculpted midriff showed a bit when he did that. Vintage t-shirts didn't cover much.

"Penn must have figured it out from the short time that passed between your tour of the lab, which is probably rare, and the robot going missing and ending up in Stella's hospital room," Jonas said. "Come on, we already know what we're going to do, so let's just do it."

"Maybe you should hang back?" I suggested. "Penn doesn't seem to know about you."

"I'm going to be brave like Obie is." Jonas winked at me, and my stomach fluttered. "Let's just go," he said, tucking his necklace into his shirt.

We met at a picnic table not too far from where Stella had fallen. Penn was wearing a light blue shirt with a collar tucked into khaki pants, and sandals with socks. He smiled when he saw us and revealed that his teeth were in place.

"So, are you the surgeon?" he asked me when we sat down.

I stared at him with my hands pressed against the bench on either side of my body. I'm pretty sure they would have been stuck there if Jonas hadn't picked one up and held it. Instead of reassuring me, like he'd probably intended, it only made me more nervous. *Was my hand sticky?*

"Please tell us what happened with Stella." I had to know what came about after I left.

"Stella woke up and eventually started talking. Her intracranial pressure is stable, her axonal disruption is less severe than before." I must have looked confused because he glanced at me and then said, "In brief, these are good signs of healing. Also, she can use all the parts—arms, legs, toes—that worked before, and she can remember that she moved them and in what order. That is a big deal."

"What happens now?" Mateo questioned. I am not sure if he meant to Stella or us.

"Well, she'll be monitored and hopefully released. Maybe she'll live a normal life, but since she wasn't really my patient, I can't make an informed prediction. Too bad you three can't get credit for your work. It was pretty fantastic, but I don't think the hospital wants to admit what happened any more than you want to come forward and say what you did. I, for one, am too old and too interested in the case and outcome to call the police or anything."

I exhaled with relief.

Penn leaned forward and clasped his hands, looking at Mateo. "You deceived me. I thought you were interested in science."

"Sir, I am sorry, but I was truly interested in science when I approached you. Probably more than I ever have been," Mateo answered. He was speaking in the manner he used when his father caught him coming home past curfew.

"What I'd really like to know," Penn continued, "is what was chasing you? What made three young people decide to steal a robot and use it to operate on a patient?"

We filled him in, starting with the shooting, then Stella's fall and her mom overhearing us, then the threats and photos taken from inside my home.

Penn raised his eyebrows and leaned back. "I understand."

I felt even better when he said that.

"I thought it must have been something big and scary," he continued. "What I also didn't get, at first, is how you just walked in."

"I didn't get that either," I added.

"Until," Penn continued, "I looked up printed heart recipients with my signature."

"Your signature?" I asked, alarmed.

"Oh, I get it," Jonas said, mysteriously. If he hadn't been holding my hand, I'd have probably smacked him with it. "I didn't know that was done."

"Obie," Penn said, "don't look so scared."

"How do you know her name?!" Mateo asked.

"Let me explain," Penn said, holding his hands up so his palms faced us. "At first, when we began 3D printing organs, we saw two needs. One was for people who had a good organ at birth that had been damaged, maybe in an accident, and needed to be replaced. That was easy, we'd just take a sample and regrow it. The other need was people with genetic mutations that caused birth defects. That was trickier because we had to fix the defect. Your eye color," he pointed at Mateo, "was an error in genetic engineering, as I'm sure you know. And we had so much demand for organs, sometimes we made mistakes in our engineering from haste, or sometimes we bypassed the engineering altogether by using a small donation from another person who didn't have the initial defect."

"I thought organ donation went away once printing was invented?" I asked.

"Yes, organ donation went away, but smaller genetic sequences became very handy. Why invent code when a perfectly good sequence, one that exists in another human and is working well, can be used?"

"What did you mean that I had your signature?" I probed.

"Obie, I donated some of my cardiac cells to your cause. I remembered your case and looked it up when I realized your cardiac signature was approved by our security systems. I have to say, when I made the donation, I never thought it could or would be used to break into my lab fifteen years later."

I sat there trying to absorb the idea that part of this man was beating inside my chest. Nothing against him, but I didn't like it too much.

"I'd only heard of it in theory," Jonas chimed in. "I never knew it had been put into practice."

"Whenever I see those protestors . . ." Penn continued. "What are they called, Humanoids?"

"Humanists," Mateo corrected.

"Whatever. They have all these posters showing man turning into machine, and they're afraid of that when they should really be looking at the person next to them. I mean, I put part of myself, a very, very small part, into another person to fix them up a bit."

"I guess I should say thanks?" I asked.

"No need but you're welcome. Stella should say thanks to you." Penn chuckled. "I wonder what Sarah would say."

"Sarah?" I asked.

"Sarah Stein, your friend, was also my friend back in the day. I worked with her at the hospital and actually had a huge crush on her, but she wouldn't have me." Penn smiled, then took out a laminated set of pocket photos. "Let me see . . . here we are." He handed me a photo of a man, woman, and young child. The man was clearly him but with fewer wrinkles and more hair. The woman was Mrs. Stein—gorgeous and young with dark brown hair and her bright blue eyes. And the girl was . . .

I gulped and handed it back to him. The girl had the face I'd seen in the lab, the one reflected against the glass jar holding Mrs. Stein's brain when it was being measured with light beams. "Is that Nava? Is that her daughter?"

"Yes," Penn said. "Lovely girl; her death was such a tragedy."

Now I was sure that my hand was sticky with sweat. Then my comm buzzed.

"Hey, um, I just got a message . . ." I stammered. "It's from Stella. She wants me to visit."

Penn stood. "I'll leave you to it. And again, don't worry about problems from me, I'm too old and honestly too intrigued by what you did to take any action."

Chapter 24

I decided to slip out quietly early in the morning before classes began. Mom was usually distracted with video visits, so I was surprised when she said, "Obie? Headed out?" as I slipped on my shoes. Crap.

"Aren't you working?" I asked. Probably the wrong thing to say before sneaking out.

"I thought I'd take the day off and we could spend some time together." She walked over to the couch and sat down with her forearms resting against her thighs, looking at me with the expression she gave her patients: focused and friendly. Wait, not exactly friendly. Like not naturally but intentionally friendly. Double crap. "Where are you off to?"

I opened my mouth to make up an answer and then I had this feeling like my breath got stuck in my throat before it broke free and then went more deeply into my lungs than I was used to. I looked at my mother differently and suddenly she seemed like a person. Maybe that sounds really weird, of course she was a person, she'd always been one, but possibly

167

not to me? I mean, she was just sitting there on the couch looking back at me with this really eager posture that said, "I'm trying." I thought she was probably wondering what I was all about and what my life was becoming, and then I started to wonder the same about her. And then I felt that I could not lie to her any longer, this person sitting on the couch.

"I'm going to the hospital to visit Stella. She woke up and I want to see her."

"I'll come with you."

We stood outside the building and waited for our vehicle in silence. My mom was looking off into space and frowning. I watched loose strands of her straight, silky brown hair move in the breeze and I realized how much I'd inherited my appearance from her. Her small stature and heart-shaped face could have been my mirror image in a few years. Of course, she was more graceful. Somehow her hair wasn't blowing into her mouth right now like mine always did.

"What are you thinking about?" I asked her.

"I was thinking about Stella and her mom, and how you and Stella used to be friends," she answered, looking back at me. Her brown eyes looked lighter in the morning light.

"It doesn't look like a happy memory," I tried to joke.

She took it seriously. "Honestly it wasn't. Not for me, at least."

"It wasn't?" I didn't understand how my playing with another little girl would mean anything to my mom. For a moment I thought my mom was going to lie, her brow did that

168

furrowing thing it does beforehand. But then it relaxed, and she told me.

"I didn't like her mom. I used to think she was jealous because you overshadowed Stella."

I overshadowed Stella? That green-eyed blonde-haired nymph child?! "What do you mean?"

"Well, you two were both very smart, but you were so creative and talkative, Stella less so, and there was always the technology thing."

"Technology thing?" In my mind, Stella was already being turned against science and medicine and must have been saying so and making my parents mad.

"Yes, Stella's parents never set limits on how much time she spent in VR, and I really wanted you to use your hands and your mind and play in the real world together." My mom sipped her coffee. Our vehicle arrived and we got in and waited for it to take off. "Sometimes I thought they let her go in VR so she'd stop fighting them."

"Fighting?"

"Yup. There was a lot of fighting in that family. I thought Stella wanted to avoid them that way, really, by going virtual."

I wondered why Stella was fighting with her parents. It seemed like they owned her now, like they set every action she took.

"And every time I suggested we get you two to cut back," my mom continued, "Stella's mom said things like, 'Mira, you have no idea what you're talking about! VR is great for parents and kids!' and I always felt like she was insulting my intelligence."

169

I was surprised because I'd never imagined my mom could feel insulted. I mean, who could ever put down my mom?

My mom kept reminiscing, glancing quickly out the window as if she were reviewing the scenes of our life on the streets below, then looking down at her fingers pressed against her coffee. "Then she started organizing VR playgroups and not inviting you, not even mentioning it."

"We got ditched?"

"Well," my mom smirked, "attempted ditching did take place. But I invited all those kids to our House for an in-person playdate, made sure to include Stella, and all the kids came except for her. And all their moms or dads told me how much fun they'd heard it was."

"And Stella just escaped into VR?"

"Obie," my mom looked at me, "this story gets pretty weird." I leaned forward. "I followed Stella into VR using my own avatar."

"You did? Why?"

"Because I wanted to see what you two were doing in there, what it was and why her mom couldn't just stop it in favor of actual finger painting or something."

My mom was a detective! She was on a mission!

"What did you find?" I tried to remember what we used to do as kids but was blank. Card games? Checkers where you go to pretend you were standing on the board instead of the pieces?

"Stella's mom had an avatar. It looked like you."

"WHAT?!"

My mom nodded. Her expression was serious, without a hint of a smile. "Yes. Her avatar looked like a little girl of Asian and Caucasian heritage with long brown hair."

I shivered and wiped my hands on my legs. This family was seriously disturbing.

"It got stranger," my mom went on. "Let's say I got you a new scarf and it had red flowers on it. The avatar would get one too, with yellow flowers. You went ice skating, so did she; your tights were purple with happy faces on the knees, hers were red with happy faces."

"What the heck? Why would she do that?" I clutched my stomach and felt it gurgle. "That is biza-zero."

"And pathetic," my mom added. "Her avatar kept approaching Stella's and trying to socialize. Stella never played with it."

"You mean Stella's mom wanted to be friends with Stella in VR?" I asked.

"I think so," my mom said. "At a certain point I stopped asking myself why and realized I needed to take action, whether I understood her or not."

"So, what did you do?"

"Oh, everything. I contacted the VR platform and complained that my daughter was being impersonated online."

"So, they stopped her?"

"No, they said there was freedom of artistic expression. So, I argued. A lot."

"Did you win?"

My mom looked at me with her brows raised as if to ask, "Do I ever lose?" I felt a little bad for even asking.

"Yes," she paused, then grinned. "Actually, I met the CEO."

"How'd you do that?" This story was better than any of those broadcasts I listened to where people shared tall tales of travel adventures or close calls with wildlife. My mom was unstoppable.

"It was tricky. I had to pose as you in VR on the platform, but I was really posing as you posing as her posing as you. Or maybe it was as her posing as you being you. It didn't really matter since everyone was the same." The vehicle seat beeped to tell me to slide back for safety. I must have been sitting on the edge without realizing.

My mom continued, "Then I went to a 'meet the CEO in the flesh' event. When I went, I brought you with me and showed him how close the resemblances were."

I thought for a moment and felt it click in my mind. "You mean, you tricked him into thinking I was Stella's mom's avatar."

"Yes. I did." My mom nodded and her voice didn't even change. If I'd done anything that clever, I would have shrieked and clapped my hands. "If the CEO thought you two were the same, how could he argue that she wasn't stealing your identity, or your future online identity?"

"So, what happened?" I was gleefully picturing Stella's mom crying as she was confronted with her corruption. It was really satisfying.

"They contacted her, and I don't know what they said but she deleted her profile."

"But what did she say?" I wanted to hear about how she'd wailed.

"Nothing."

"Nothing?"

"I never told her what I did. She only heard from the corporation. We never spoke of it, and I still don't know if she found out how this huge VR platform knew she was stealing an identity and whose it was."

"You really never told her?"

"All I wanted was for her to stop. And I was so relieved when Stella stopped going to your school and just drifted off. Oh, my goodness was I ever." My mom sighed and rested her head against the back of the seat. I sat there frustrated because I didn't get the satisfying ending I'd wanted, but also super impressed. My mom was like a noble knight on an electronic stallion who only operated in darkness. I still had one question left, though.

"But why do you think she did that—mimicked me in her virtual self?" I asked as the vehicle landed at the hospital and we got out. "To connect with Stella in VR you could pose as any kid."

"Honestly, I think she needed you, or someone just like you, in order for the whole thing to work."

"But . . . why?"

My mom put her arm around my shoulder. "You were best friends with her daughter. And she really missed her daughter."

And just then it hit me—how lucky I was to have my mom. I mean, we did things together all the time and I'd never even thought that was anything special or rare. Plus, I'd always supposed my dad was the one who knew how to solve problems. Every time I got an A grade, I decided it had been because he'd helped me out, as much as I didn't like his lectures. Had my mom been sitting there the whole time, teaching me too? How had I missed this?

We knocked softly on the door. Stella's mom opened it and I felt my pulse speed up.

"What are you . . .? Oh, hello." She stepped into the hallway instead of backward to let us into the hospital room. I was glad I'd brought my mom. "Mira, it has been such a long time."

My mom held up the treats we'd brought. "We won't stay long, we just want to extend our well wishes, if that's okay."

"Actually, this isn't a great time. Stella needs to rest."

"We understand," my mom started. "Perhaps we could give these cookies to you, and you could give them to her."

"Stella isn't supposed to eat sweets now as part of her recovery," her mom said, holding her palms out against the box.

My mom raised an eyebrow. I bet this little lie went against her clinical training. Sweets were always part of my recovery from anything.

"I invited them, Mom," Stella said softly but clearly from inside the room. "Please let them in." There was an awkward pause where I bet her mom was debating whether to let us in or grab the cookies and break the box over our heads. "Mom, I want to see them," Stella insisted.

As her mom stepped aside, we slowly entered the room and I looked at my patient for the first time since the surgery. She was lying in the hospital bed, propped up by maybe ten pillows and twenty soft toy animals. I could picture her mom inserting each one into every gap between Stella's body and the mattress. She left her head on the pillow as she looked at me. Her face appeared lined with fatigue and there were dark circles beneath her eyes. Her head was wrapped in a pink cloth with a flamingo pattern. The enforced cheeriness of the decoration made the atmosphere seem even more morbid. But at least her green eyes were alert as they focused on me. In spite of everything—like Stella's irrational fear of me, her role in spreading hatred and harm, and the way her parents had blackmailed me—it was a relief to see and hear her.

"Hello," Stella said gently. I remained silent. Again, my dad had always been into the "Don't say it until you know what it is," motto. I certainly didn't know what to say here.

"We brought cookies," my mom announced, setting the box on her side table.

"Thank you," Stella said, looking at her, then me. "It is truly nice of you to come." *Truly? Was that something sick people said in hospitals?* I stood a few feet away from her bed awkwardly.

"So, how are you doing today?" I asked. I thought that was what my mom usually asked her patients.

Stella teared up. "Obie," she stammered, "I don't know what to say."

175

"Honey, you've been through a lot," her mom piped up. She'd been leaning against the window and watching me like I was about to steal the bed sheets. "I'm sure this is just from the trauma of your injury, and you'll recover from it well."

"I'm sorry," Stella said, wiping her eyes. "I'm just so emotional all the time."

"You don't have to be sorry for anything," my mom said, reaching out as if to pat her hand, then looking at Stella's mom and letting her hand drop by her side. "We are just happy to see you as you are. Would you like a cookie?" She opened the box, confirming to me that sweets were an acceptable part of recovery.

"Rugelach!" Stella squealed. "I love these!" She picked one up and took a small bite that she chewed as if relishing air after being briefly suffocated. Weird.

"I'm glad you like them so much," my mom said. "I wasn't sure if they'd be . . . right for you, so we bought a mix."

"You did just right," Stella said. "I've loved these since I was a girl." Her mom looked at her with one eyebrow raised, then actually shot me a look as if I would know what Stella was talking about. I shrugged my shoulders. If we'd eaten rugelach together as kids, I couldn't remember. Sharing any of Mrs. Stein's homemade baked goods with anyone other than my mom seemed really unlikely, but maybe I was a nicer kid than I could recall.

My mom and Stella's mom stood awkwardly next to one another. My mom stood like a warrior princess balancing a crown on her head and a spear on her shoulder. Stella's mom stood like a shriveled desert cactus gasping for water. I looked

176

at Stella to see if she wanted to talk, to say anything to break this silence—even an unpleasant word or two about the argument on the bridge before her fall. She just finished chewing her cookies, gazed into space, then yawned and leaned her head back.

"That's our cue to leave," my mom said. Stella's mom didn't argue, and we walked ourselves to the door.

"Thank you again for coming," Stella said, closing her eyes. I felt pretty satisfied with the visit, as awkward as it was at moments. Maybe life could just go back to normal now. Then Stella opened her eyes and added, "Such a dearie." The words were quiet but clear just before she closed her eyes and fell asleep. I realized that normal would be impossible.

"That was . . . an odd conversation to have with Stella," my mom said to me in the hall. I remained silent, not because I wanted to withhold information from her, but because my mouth had gone totally numb, possibly my mind too. No one called me "dearie." No one except Mrs. Stein.

177

Chapter 25

"You mean to tell me she acted like Mrs. Stein? She was probably really tired and that made her seem old," Mateo said. We were sitting in Jonas' lab, on large lumps he called "bean bag chairs."

"No, it was more than that. She called me 'dearie.' And she said she liked the rugelach and always had, ever since we were kids. I actually had House search all the photos I had from when Stella and I used to play together, and I didn't spot a single cookie of any kind." That was true and reminded me that her parents had been really insistent our snacks be fruit or whatever protein mix was on trend at the time, like seaweed and tofu blended into ionized water.

"It is totally possible," Jonas said. He was crouching on the edge of my bean bag, and I could see a small, dark trail of hair on his lower back. It was pretty intriguing. "I mean, we did take part of one person and put it into the other. And that part had a lot to do with memory. Did the hospital say anything about how the hole in Stella's brain seemed to not grow back and then to grow back all of a sudden?"

"Not that her mom mentioned."

"Do you think her mom thought anything was wrong?"

"Maybe . . . although maybe she thought it was general waking-up-after-brain-damage stuff."

"Who cares?" Mateo chimed in. "I mean, Stella's awake. No one is going to know what we did. Penn said he'd keep quiet, and Obie wasn't identified another way."

"I just feel funny that I changed another person," I tried to explain. "It's like I should take another step and I don't know in what direction." It was true. Everything had become a *now-what?* or a *how-do-I?* I mean, I had to design a science experiment for school. What was I supposed to come up with after all that?

"Forgive me if I don't feel sorry for the person who probably helped arranged my shooting," Mateo retorted.

"I don't feel sorry for her..." I realized I was stammering. "I think I feel responsible for her." When I was a kid, I'd once broken the leg off my toy doll. My parents, being what they are, hadn't allowed me to use tech to fix her. I'd had to figure it out myself and ended up with my dad watching for safety while I used glue and heat to stick her limb back onto her body. My dad had smiled and clapped me on the back, then gone to bed. I, however, had stayed up all night checking on my doll, afraid that she was in pain, or her leg would fall off again. Going from that to a brain transplant was like transitioning from running through sprinklers to jumping off an airplane into a waterfall over the ocean.

"I want to think this over," Jonas said, standing up and breaking off my reverie. "And I need to get to work. I've got customers coming in search of really high waisted jeans today."

Mateo and I headed to his place and sat on the back deck where I soaked in some sun and tried to relax.

"So, how's it going with dream boy?" he asked me as he started pulling up weeds and watering the flower beds.

"Well, he's cute and smart and I've stopped noticing that his t-shirts have the stitching on the outside."

Mateo snorted. "What do you think of his business? With all those organs coming out of his lab?"

I shrugged. "It helped when we need it, I guess." It actually made me a bit uncomfortable, but I figured it wasn't my business now that Mateo had his spleen. "Do you think Jonas is a mad scientist?" I asked.

Mateo paused. "No, I don't. I think he's brilliant and that he misses his mother a lot, or else he wouldn't touch that necklace with her DNA in it all the time."

"Me too."

"You guys kiss yet?"

"No!" I blushed. "When would we have done that, while we were preparing to break into a hospital?"

"Sounds like a good time to me," Mateo said.

I snorted.

"I think he's a little scared of you, Obie."

"Of me?"

"Yes, *mi amiga*. Don't think that he is perfect and put him on a pedestal and all that. You deserve your own."

"Thanks." That was nice. I watched Mateo for a few minutes, noticing the way his hands moved with self-assurance. They didn't hover or change direction once they'd started out one way, they just dove into the soil and completed their mission.

"Don't you want to relax?" I asked him.

"I am relaxing," he answered without looking up. He was cupping a purple flower head in his palm and gently pulling away the dried leaves on the stem below. I didn't think my hands had ever done anything so delicately. Not even brain surgery.

"I never knew you liked to garden for fun." I wondered how I'd missed this in the years I'd known him.

"I'm doing it more at home now." He paused. "I stopped volunteering."

"You did what? You stopped?" I sat forward. This was huge. Mateo had been volunteering for years and in so many places with so many tasks that they'd blended in my mind. Along the way I'd switched from asking him "How was the beach cleanup/canned food drive/building painting/etc.?" to "How was it?" and leaving off any specifics.

"Yes," was all he said. He pulled a weed and tapped it against the ground, shaking off soil stuck to the roots.

"How . . . did you come to that decision?"

"I just decided to stop. I'm done." He kept his head turned away from me. I could only see the backs of his wide ears.

181

"Not that I'm not happy for you, but wasn't that a big part of your, um—" I gave a quick mental scan for the right word. Identity? Value system? "Your deal?"

"I'm still not into freebies because I don't think anything is free, and I don't want to live off others. But the government gave me an out because of the shooting and I took it." He changed from a squat to resting on one leg and gazing downwards. I didn't ask the question of why. I knew he'd tell me anyway. "I have given enough. And I can get what I need out of this," he added, gesturing behind him at the flowers. They rippled in a breeze as if in response.

"What do you need?" I'd always thought of his volunteering as sucking resources out of him, not as a symbiotic relationship.

"It made me feel good to earn my organs, but also to build something. I got to look back at the beach or park or whatever and say, 'I did that, I made it what it is.'"

I didn't know what to say.

"How can anyone look down on me rightfully when I can create such things, Obie? They can't. I know what I can do." He projected his comm onto the wall and started showing me images of gorgeous gardens with flowers. They flowed somehow, by height maybe, or texture, or color, or all three. The landscape went way beyond a simple set of potted plants presented in rows. It was textured in a way that made sense, that fit the background environment but had its own unique message. He flipped to photos of beaches he'd cleaned. The before photos were crowded with trash; the after photos showed pure sand with sculptures placed perfectly along the seaside. Each was made of metal and broken glass woven together in a way that reminded me of a vine reaching up, growing over a fence, and sprouting into the sky. They looked like an extension of the boulders and rocks behind them, but again they didn't match completely and stood out as their own statement. It was a declaration of beauty. I exist. I am possible.

"Did you build those out of the trash you picked up?" I asked in awe.

"Yes," he answered, smiling.

"Does anyone else know? I mean, these are amazing. The whole world should know about them."

"I've just started posting them. The response has been really good. I think I'm getting an Israeli fan base," he laughed a little. "And one of the other volunteers from my group wants to connect me with her friend in landscape architecture."

I thought I'd known everything about Mateo that there was to know and could not believe he'd done this without me. Then I shook my head. We'd come so far since he was attacked by that drone at school. This was great.

"Mateo, I am so happy for you. I just can't believe you got so much from volunteering. I mean, wow!"

"Well," he looked up at me, "there's a bit more to it."

"What else?"

"I started to use the EmpathSpin app a bit," he admitted. His parents let him and mine didn't!? Dang it.

"How did that go?" I was really curious but also nervous. The stories I'd heard were pretty dirty. Like you'd drop in, see the bathroom floor, and then realize someone was sitting on the toilet, doing their business and sharing it with you.

"Obie, it's amazing. I've been straight, Caucasian, female—you name it and in any combination."

"And?"

"Well, I used to wonder if people were being mean to me. Not people who threw trash at me, that was obvious, but the regular stuff—buying things near me at stores, using the same table at the library."

"I don't understand," I said.

"You know, someone says, 'have a nice day' and you wonder if they're really being sarcastic because they hate you, but you can't tell for sure?"

I shook my head no.

"Okay, I guess you'd have to be uncloseted about your heart to know what I mean. Anyway, I realized that most people are good. Just people, going about their day." He pantomimed walking with two of his fingers in the air.

"I guess that's reassuring?" I wondered aloud.

"Yeah, well, the other thing I noticed was that, when people seemed mean, it was mostly because they were dumb, not bad." He rubbed some dirt between his fingers and went on. "Like this one woman, I think she was in her sixties, was playing tennis with her friend—some guy who was older than her but beating her at the game. I was in her eyes while they played, and we were losing! Anyway, she made some joke about how he'd probably been reworked to be genetically superior. I can't remember exactly what she said."

I stiffened. The genetic superiority thing was a common insult we organ recipients ran into. It was from the idea that we hadn't been fixed but improved beyond normal human nature.

"I know, right?" Mateo said, probably noticing my posture. "So, I took a risk and left her a note about it in the app. It was pretty weird: 'Thanks for letting me be part of you today, by the way it is a common misconception that organ recipients are genetically superior. We just get our defects fixed and we're brought back to neutral, nothing more.'"

"Well said," I told him.

"Thank you. So, she replied in less than an hour and said she was so sorry. She'd known that organ recipients were just medically treated but had not known that comment she'd made tied back to discrimination and fear about us. She was so nice about it; she actually thanked me for letting her know and then told me how much she'd enjoyed building a sculpture through my eyes. Then we wrote back and forth about art for a while. She'd like to come to an exhibit of mine if I ever have one."

"That's incredible." I had goosebumps. And slight envy that a random person had known my best friend's artistic side before me. I wondered what Mrs. Stein would think of the EmpathSpin App. I thought she would have liked it because it humanized the other side when all the Humanists were trying to dehumanize others.

"Don't worry, I'll make sure to invite you to my exhibit too," Mateo said, wryly, his blue eye sparkling, his tan ears sticking out.

I laughed and then leaned forward and hugged him. He smelled like the soil.

"Hey, Obie," he said, squeezing me back. "It was a wonderful thing and I'm glad I can tell you that most people are wonderful too."

That afternoon I got a message from Jonas.

"I am stalking the patient from a distance," he wrote, "and she happens to be alone in the hospital garden, no parents around. Care to join me for some spying?"

Honestly, I had no plans or desire to go back to see Stella but the invitation from Jonas changed all that. I arrived at the hospital wearing the fan-hat that I'd bought at Jonas' store for laughs but also as a slight disguise. The bill covered my head better than anything else I owned, and Stella was in the hospital garden I'd run through after her surgery. People were sitting outside and enjoying the sunshine. I found Jonas peering around the corner of a wall.

"She looks so sad," he said, pointing. Stella, her head wrapped in that flamingo cloth, was sitting in lotus position like a Buddha statue on a bench. She was gazing at her palms as if they were strange to her, her mouth in a slight frown.

"Should we talk to her?" he asked me.

"Why?"

"Honestly because I'm really, really curious," he answered.

I nodded and we walked slowly over.

"Hi," I said.

Stella looked up. "Hi, Obie!" Her voice sounded artificially high pitched.

186

"This is my Jonas." I meant to say friend, as in my friend, Jonas, and felt heat rise up my neck into my face. Maybe wearing the fan-hat had been a good idea.

"Hi, Stella. I've heard so much about you. I'm glad you're up and about," Jonas said. Perfectly.

"Oh, I hope only the good things," Stella said, weakly smiling. "You two want to sit down?"

I sat next to her, and Jonas sat on the grass in front of us. He looked at Stella intently. I felt my chest tighten a bit with jealousy.

"So, how do you two know each other?" Stella asked. She sounded normal for a moment, like we were gossiping during a sleep over.

"Jonas runs a retail store I like to visit," I answered. Because I went organ shopping there.

"Oh, how neat," she smiled. "Is that where you bought that hat?"

"Hey, we offer a strong commitment to functional fashion," Jonas said. Stella laughed. I kept a straight face but grimaced inwardly.

"Sorry I didn't bring cookies this time," I said.

"Cookies?" she looked confused. "Oh, that's okay, I ate so many last time."

We sat there quietly for a moment and then Jonas looked at me as if to say, *Are you going to investigate this? Because I can't.*

"I was wondering how you were doing," I broached. "Last time, I felt pretty . . . uncertain. And I didn't know if you wanted to talk about your fall. I was there, I don't know if you remember."

187

Stella's eyes darkened. "I remember," she said. "I was afraid, and then I backed up and fell, but I don't know why I was so scared. You were there and my parents and some birds."

I stayed quiet. I didn't want to remind her she was afraid of me and that's why she had her accident. I didn't want her to be scared now, or to feel stupid, which the whole thing really was. She may have helped shoot my best friend, but all I could see was how she looked like a small kid wearing a lame flamingo head wrap and looking lost in a garden.

"Honestly, the more I try to remember about the past," she went on, "I just feel so sad."

"Sad?" I probed.

"Yes. Sad in a heavy and homesick way. Sad in a way that's like when a beloved pet dies, only worse because it radiates from the center of my being."

Jonas raised his eyebrows at me. He'd never met Mrs. Stein, but I thought he was getting a strong sign that post-surgery Stella didn't speak like anyone near our age.

"I'm sorry to hear that," I offered.

"But the thing is," Stella continued, her tears falling. "For some reason, I hope to always feel this way . . . it's as if I'd miss the missing. I want to remember it forever, even if it is sad." She looked at me with a piercing gaze that felt weirdly familiar. I felt goosebumps break out on my shoulders and I crossed my arms to rub some warmth into myself. Then Stella shut her eyes, sighed, and looked back at me. She smiled in the way she used to when we played games as kids, back when things were relatively innocent. She looked like she'd just discovered chocolate for the first time in her life. I calmed a bit, but the switch was weird too.

Stella wiped her eyes with her hands, looked around, maybe for a tissue, and then pulled at the flamingo wrap around her head. As it unraveled, it revealed Stella's familiar and bare head. It was still shaven but with bits of blonde fuzz showing here and there above her ears. At the top near her forehead, I could see the clear stitches I'd used to sew the cover back into place above her skull. Her skin was already beginning to grow over the white patch. I could see the pink tentacles of her dermis reaching out from the edges of the circle, trying to hold hands with each other but too far apart. A few people in the garden glanced at her.

She dried her eyes with the flamingo cloth and said, "Sometimes at night I dream about a little girl. She isn't me, but she is like me, and I don't really know who she is, but when I wake up somehow, I miss her so much that I don't want to let go of the dream." Then she picked up the flamingo wrap and started to cry into it again. Another mood swing. Without thinking, I reached for her hand and held it. I didn't know if I was comforting her, Mrs. Stein, or myself, but I think it was a combination of the three of us. I looked at Jonas, and he stood and walked away to give us space.

"Obie," Stella said, lowering her voice to a whisper, "I remember why I was afraid of you on the bridge." She glanced toward Jonas, now perusing the flower bushes a ways away. "I just didn't know if he knew or not."

I straightened. She remembered my heart. "Are you still afraid of me?"

189

"No," she answered.

I wasn't relieved, I was only intrigued. Was she actually looking out for me in case Jonas was a Humanist? Then I remembered how I'd told Jonas that my heart was 3D printed and how he didn't care at all. It made me feel good—better than realizing Stella was actually looking out for me now.

"Obie," Stella sighed. "Obie, I can remember everything. And I know what my parents did, and I don't know what to do."

"What do you mean you know what they did?"

"With the shooting where Mateo was hurt." She stopped abruptly and I wondered if she thought I was wearing a secret recorder.

We sat silently. What could I have said to the daughter of murderers? Then she went on, "I just don't know what to do. Who would take care of me?"

"What do you mean?"

"If . . . say that people found out what they did and then they went away . . . what would happen to me? Especially now?"

I know it sounds selfish, but what I thought of right then was more *What am I supposed to do?* than *Poor thing, what can she do?* It was like I'd adopted a child, or adopted their problem in a way, and I kept telling myself it wasn't really mine, but I wasn't so sure.

Stella and I both heard a loud *thwack*! We turned to see Jonas a few feet away, crouching in the bushes, staring intently at the leaves as if that had been all he'd been doing. I was pretty sure he'd been hiding in them to eavesdrop and let go of the tall branches too quickly.

"I'll come back, Stella," I said. "I need to think."

She thanked me, leaned forward as if to hug me, changed her mind, and awkwardly went back into the hospital building.

"Jonas, you won't believe—" I started.

"I know," Jonas said. "I heard everything. And, man can those stems really snap back hard." He rubbed the side of his face where I noticed a red line along his cheek. There were a few petals in his hair too. As stressed as I was, it was pretty funny, and I laughed really hard.

"Jonas, we need to send you to spy training school," I managed to say while giggling.

"Hey, at least I'm not wearing a hat with a fan as my disguise," he protested, but he was laughing too. He reached forward and I thought he was going to spin the fan for me, so I stood with my face upturned, ready to receive this punishment, and then he kissed me. Like, put his hand on the back of my neck, leaned forward, and planted a very soft but firm kiss right on my mouth. It lasted for more than four seconds. I know because I started counting after at least a few, and it shot energy into my knees and made my stomach warm. So warm, maybe that's why my fan-hat turned on, blowing the petals off his hair, and making us both laugh again.

Chapter 26

I got home in a trance of glee. I'd reenacted the whole thing in my head about a hundred times on the way home and each time chose to recall a different point more strongly, like the way his eyes had sparkled afterwards, or the way his fingers had felt on my neck. My lips still felt tingly where he'd kissed me. I wondered how long he'd noticed me in that way and if it had been right away, like it had been for me, or if it had been spontaneous and hit him all at once at that moment in the garden.

My parents were sitting on the couch and stopped talking when I walked in.

"Hello!" I said, helping myself to some lemonade. "I'm going to do some homework in my room."

"Obie," my mom said, "we'd like to talk."

"Alright, but can we talk tomorrow? I have so much to do." Like call Mateo right now and tell him what happened.

"Obie," my dad said. *Uh-oh*, I thought.

"I really need to study," I said, trying to sound authoritative and like I wasn't lying.

"Obie," my mom said.

I sat down. House extended my leg rest.

"Honey, we can tell that something is going on and we want to know what it is," my dad said.

"We're not angry but worried," my mom added.

"What do you mean?" I asked, trying to buy some time to think.

"You've been very distant recently," my mom said.

"And many . . . events have taken place as of late that could cause stress. Sometimes stress causes action. Other times, lack of action," my dad said.

"I don't understand," I said.

"Obie, your habits have changed, and we want to make sure you aren't doing, or not doing, anything you might regret later on," my mom explained.

"My habits have changed?"

"Besides the staring off into the horizon," my dad answered, "you have been getting up . . . um, early."

"You know when I've been getting up?"

"Obie," my mom said in her cutting-to-the-chase voice, "we checked with House because we were worried. You left the building really early one morning wearing a blonde wig."

"YOU ASKED HOUSE?" What the heck?! "You snooped on me?!" I was so angry I stood up before House could retract the footrest and fell forward. House raised the armrest to catch me.

"We thought maybe it had to do with that boy who was on the roof with you and Mateo," my dad said in a pleading tone.

That boy!

"But then that visit with Stella at the hospital," my mom explained, "it just didn't feel right to me. Not as a nurse and not as a mother. So, we thought we'd just ask you. Because we do trust you, Obie, to make the right decisions. And because we want to help our daughter when she's going through troublesome times."

"But you . . ." I was livid. "You violated . . . I don't like this." Especially the fact that they were right. I was going through troublesome times, and I had been making decisions and taking action. "You trust me, but you used House to spy on me!" All of the warmth leftover from Jonas' kiss pooled down my body and into a hot pile of anger in my knees.

"Honey," my dad said, "you have to—"

"Don't call me honey!"

"Stop yelling," my mom said.

"I am not yelling! I am not yelling!"

"You need to understand that it's our job to guide and protect you," my dad explained. "That is our number one task. And if that boy was leading you down a bad path, we couldn't let that happen."

That boy?! Again?! Enough with this!

I turned and ran into my room and tried to slam the door behind me but it slowed down to create a soft close, so I pulled on the doorknob, my heels braced against the ground. This made no difference and I just sort of swung there.

"Obie," House said, "is there a problem?"

"CLOSE THE DOOR. JUST CLOSE THE DANG DOOR."

The door closed quickly but without slamming. It just made a neat little "click." That was even more obnoxious. I needed somewhere to put all of my rage. *How dare they? Do they have any idea the stress I am under?*

I knelt beside my bed and burrowed my face into my mattress while slamming my fists and screaming. That turned on the massage function which pulsated against my mouth and made my voice vibrate. I rolled onto my back and kicked my heels against the floor, but the sound was completely absorbed by the flooring, making me feel like I was trapped in a soundproof fish tank.

"Obie, how can I help you?" House asked.

"Shut up!" I shouted. I got up and grabbed my pillow. Finally, something I can use, my last resource.

I raised my pillow above my head as if it were a sacrificial offering to the ceiling, then brought it down with all my strength. It got caught on my lighting display, but when I wrangled it free, I still managed to make a loud *thud* when my pillow hit my bed. It was the most delicious sound I'd ever heard. I crawled into a fetal position on top and started crying with a mixture of relief and frustration, but mostly frustration.

About ten minutes later I heard a knock.

"Obie?" my mom said from outside the door.

I didn't answer.

"Hon, um, Obie, we made dinner. Tomato salad! And freshly baked bread!" My dad sounded nervous in a pathetic way. It was kind of touching. I sat up and told House to open the door. My parents stood there warily. I wondered how I looked to them.

"Jonas didn't mislead me. He's a good person. He isn't bad or anything you're worrying about," I said.

"Then what on earth is going on?" my mom asked.

I looked at her, then at my dad. As angry as I was, I suddenly felt like telling them how hard it had been—to have my friend shot, to have a childhood friend turn from me in fear, and to have horrible people threaten me and my family because of what kept me alive. Then to have the weight of a human brain, and really an entire human being, in my hands, and to know I'd saved a life but changed it forever in a way that I could not understand, that maybe I would never be able to.

And so, I did. I broke down and I told them everything.

Chapter 27

They didn't yell at me; I'll give them that. My dad actually started laughing.

"Did you hear that, Mira? And we were worried about boys and drugs. She was actually performing brain surgery." My mom didn't answer at first. Her face was pale, and her lips so drawn in I couldn't see them.

"He was here?" she asked. "Malloy was in our House?"

I showed her a picture of the brain image poster he'd put on the ceiling above my bed.

"Obie, you should have come to us immediately," she said, her eyes wide.

"I'm sorry," I cried. "But he was going to hurt you, and me, and I had gotten this illegal spleen for Mateo, and they were going to expose the whole thing."

"One crime begets another," my dad said. He was standing, looking out my window with his hands clasped behind his back.

"I can't believe this. I knew we should have gotten involved earlier," my mom started ranting. She turned to my dad. "David, now isn't the time to get philosophical."

He turned to face her. I inhaled. "You're right," he said. I exhaled. "We need to take stock of where we are. No looking back, no what-ifs and how-comes. As far as that goes," he looked at me, "I understand why you did what you did."

"Because they scared her! They came in here and they threatened her!" My mom apparently wasn't done looking back quite yet. "I NEVER liked Stella's parents. This is their revenge against us for that VR stupidity! House!"

"Yes."

"How did you let this happen?!" my mom asked.

"Malloy entered with credentials—"

"Shut up, House! Just shut up!" Mom screamed.

I felt pretty badly for House right then, even though I knew that Houses couldn't feel; they could only learn from error and grow that way.

"Mira, it was another hacking. It wasn't House's fault." My dad walked over to my mom. He put his hands above her shoulders, saw her expression, and then let them drop by his sides. "We need to assess where we are and what to do now."

"Go ahead," my mom said, sitting down at my desk and crossing her arms over her chest. Then she stood up again. "You know what? I am done. Just done for now. You figure this out," she commanded my dad, then turned and walked into their room. I wondered if she wished she could slam the door.

In the silence that followed, I realized I was starving. I ambled into the kitchen and pulled a fistful of bread off the loaf on the counter. My dad came over to join me.

"We need to think about how to keep this quiet," he said. His expression seemed thoughtful, and his gaze was directed above my head and out the window. "I don't believe that you can be connected to the surgery. I think the point this Penn character made about not wanting to admit what you were able to do is valid. The hospital would get into trouble. And if this story ever did come out, it is clear you were threatened. We have the record from House, and we have the photo of the poster Malloy put above your bed."

I stuffed my face with bread and nodded.

"The next question is what to do now about Stella's parents. You and your . . . friends held up your end of the bargain. You 'fixed' Stella and should be left alone now," he said, using air quotes. "But that doesn't mean her parents will stop feeling angry towards you, and they may be even angrier when they realize their daughter hasn't been returned in the exact condition she was in before she fell."

"It's all their fault," I pouted. "If they hadn't been such crappy, hateful people, none of this would have happened. No shooting. No spleen damage. Stella wouldn't have even fallen off the bridge because she was afraid of me."

"True," my dad said, reaching for my bread and taking a pinch. "So, what we need to think about is how they can be stopped in the event they wish to cause harm again."

"There's one more thing," I suggested, feeling uneasy.

"What's that?"

"Stella said she was thinking of turning them in when I talked to her in the garden. She just wasn't sure what would happen to her if she did."

"And that's one more question to add to the pile to think about. But now I need to check on your mother," my dad said. He patted my shoulder, stood, and left. I didn't mind; comfort food was all I wanted right then.

"Are you having trouble sleeping again, Ba??" House asked.

"There's just too much to think about," I answered. It was true—brain transplants, memory transplants, changes in personal values after a transplant, what to do next. And Jonas. And kissing.

"Ba, I wanted again to express how sorry I am about the break in."

"That's okay, House. You were hacked. And you protected us as much as you could by not letting Malloy access the Central System."

"I've made sure he will never hurt you again."

"Good. I'm going to get up for some warm milk."

House turned the lights on low and I padded into the kitchen. My dad was sitting at the table, staring out the window.

"Heya," he said. "Can't sleep either?"

"No." I sat down across from him. House heated up a pan for my milk. "How's mom?"

"She's asleep."

I nodded.

200

"So," my dad asked, "is Jonas your boyfriend?"

"Um, I'm not sure."

"Do you want him to be?"

"Maybe." I stood to get my milk. It was a good way to get out of this conversation.

"Can I ask you a question?" my dad asked when I got back. "I hope it isn't too awkward."

"Yeah, okay."

"Are Jonas' pants sweats or just regular pants and why do they look so strange grabbing his ankles like that?"

I giggled. "Dad, that's vintage."

"Is it really?"

"Yes, he runs a store with clothes from 2020," I informed him.

"And prints spleens?"

"Yes, in the basement."

"Ah, good to diversify the revenue streams. Dress your customers on the inside and out."

I giggled again.

"Is he nice to you, this boy?" my dad wanted to know.

"Yeah, he's nice to me." He was. Very nice.

My dad leaned forward, pressed my elbow with his on the table, and blew his light brown hair out of his eyes. "If not, I want to hear about it."

"Okay."

"I've also been thinking about Mrs. Stein," my dad said. He leaned back and clasped his hands behind his chair, stretching his shoulders. "I'm not sure if to say you transplanted empathy or made it irrelevant because part of

Sarah Stein can literally live in the skin of another, and Stella can actually experience another person."

"Maybe both?" I asked. "Did you know that was even possible?"

"Well," he again focused on the space behind my head. "I knew this was what we policy employees were trying to avoid when we made brain transplants and printing illegal. Too much playing around with what people were made from. I was always disappointed, in a way, by that."

"Why?"

"Because human learning is limited. Every scientist must train for years to learn what others discovered before them, and only then do they really get to explore further, to find the new frontier."

"I don't understand."

"What I'm saying is that, if we could transplant the knowledge and skills of one old and experienced person into the next generation, they could accomplish more than ever. It would be like mimicking evolution and passing along what helped us, not just to survive, but to thrive," he cleared his throat. "And the effects we'd pass along would go beyond our height or ability to digest certain foods or how to best react to stress." He waved his hand around as if dismissing a silly notion.

"Why not just print brains?" I asked.

"Printing brain parts would make us lose the natural variation of the human species and replace it with our version of progress. Why invent more technology when we could use ourselves? We don't even need printing, that's just advanced photocopy machines with a bit of tinkering and improvement built in. We can take from each other. Take the good parts."

Dad stopped looking behind me and stared into my eyes. "Now, I know what you might be thinking—at some point we became too humble."

I'd actually been wondering if the milk I was drinking would make me have to pee at night and if Jonas might kiss me again the next time I saw him.

"We started using the phrase 'only human,'" he went on. "We stopped taking advantage of the natural resources around us and focused on technology. And all these people at the polls are thinking about topics like how a machine could help with their athletic ability or could make them prettier. What they need to realize is that human-to-human innovation can do things unimagined. And Humanists should be more nervous about the people around them than what's coming off the printer."

I pondered this for a moment. "Whoa."

My dad smiled. "Anyway, I like the way you explore ideas," he said. It made me feel proud to hear. "I just hope your sort-of-boyfriend can keep up," he added.

Chapter 28

"You made kissy kissy and waited until now to tell me?!" I was pretty sure Mateo was feigning indignance over the video feed I'd projected from my comm onto my bedroom ceiling.

"Yeah, but only because my parents ambushed me at home, and I had to tell them about the brain surgery first."

"Gosh, as much as I hate it when I have to explain brain surgery to my family, you still should have reported to me immediately. Even with just a graphic of two of those yellow circle happy face things smashing their mouths against each other's like they were devouring a meal. I would have understood, even with no other explanation."

"Well, it wasn't quite like that."

"Okay, so an image of two dolls having their faces pressed together by a little girl with pigtails who is laying on her floor playing with her dollhouse."

"Then you would have thought that I was some sexually frustrated little kid with deep psychological wounds."

Mateo cocked an eyebrow.

"Hey, I am not that bad!" I protested.

"Alright," he said. "No. I would have thought, 'Obie and Jonas kissed and now I can rest knowing the world turns as it should.'"

"Eh?"

"Come on, *chica*, the sexual tension had to build up to something. Even I've been breaking out into sweats at random times just from spending time with you two. Or finding myself watching old films of wild horses running through fields."

"Maybe you are the frustrated little kid with issues," I said.

"Maybe I am, but a little less so knowing that at least someone macked on that blue-eyed genius dream boy." I giggled at his words, and he went on, "Anyway, what are we going to do now? Are your parents cooking up a plan?"

"No. They said they didn't want to do anything until they knew exactly what that anything would be."

"Smart. So, we just wait?"

"Just wait."

Jonas messaged me that afternoon. "Hey."

I jumped up from my desk, ran across my room three times, lay on my back bicycling my legs into the air, then shoved my head under my pillow and squealed.

"Ba?" House asked. "Should I be worried about you?"

"I need privacy mode now, House."

"Very well," House said, turning the light above my door light gray to show I wasn't being monitored. Some parents didn't even give their kids that option. I was glad mine did.

"Hey," I wrote back, after writing out and deleting many other potential replies.

"Good news," he wrote. "My face healed from being slapped by those flowers."

"Thanks for the update. I was worried."

"Want to get some ice cream?" he asked.

"If you think you're up for it. I don't want to risk another floral assault."

"I think I can handle it if you're there to protect me from the local vegetation."

I changed my shirt three times and then made House give me a brief fashion color consultation before choosing a dark green top that would bring out some of the hazel in my eyes.

Jonas was wearing a vintage t-shirt with a peace symbol on it next to the word *out*. I decided I'd ask him what that meant later. He smiled when he saw me. One of his cheeks dimpled.

"Hey," he said.

"Hi."

He hugged me for about three seconds, then we went into the ice cream parlor and punched in our order.

"So, what do you do when your hands aren't in someone's else's skull?" Jonas asked me as the appliance churned our ingredients together.

I laughed. "Um, school. Let's see, hanging out with Mateo, doing exercise videos."

"Exercise vids alone or with Mateo?" Jonas asked, grabbing two spoons as the machine sprinkled almonds on top of our vanilla bean ice cream and pushed it onto the pick-up counter.

"Mostly alone." I didn't want to tell him I exercised with my mom and her aerobics group.

"I see. And are things like normal now?" Jonas handed me a spoon and I took a timid bite of vanilla bean. I wasn't used to sharing food this way.

"You mean post-surgery?" I asked.

"Yep. I was a wreck after my first organ printing." Jonas scooped up a large spoonful and I relaxed a bit.

"Yes . . . but there's more to it. I think everything in my life has become, 'Now what?'" I shrugged my shoulders to punctuate the phrase. "I don't know how to explain . . . I just don't know what I'm supposed to do with myself," I admitted.

"Kinda hard to come down from doing brain surgery, eh? Like you just graduated from all your medical training and now somehow, you're stuck back in high school," he suggested.

"Yeah, that, and also I feel . . . not nervous, but not relaxed either. I just feel different." It was nice how Jonas didn't interrupt me. "It's like it was weirder to see the hate coming out of Stella's parents' eyes on that bridge. More than seeing the inside of the human head." I didn't realize that was what I felt until I said it.

"I get it," Jonas said. "When I printed my first organ, I had all these ideas of what it would be like—lots of lightning bolts cracking above me like I was a mad scientist as I held a kidney in my hand, that sort of thing. And then it wasn't. But a few weeks after my first organ sale, I saw my customer on public transit. It lasted only for a minute, and I didn't talk to him, but I remember his expression."

"What was it like?" I asked, secretly admiring the way his long, dark lashes framed his eyes.

"Happy. Not like bursting with ecstasy, but just content sitting there and reading."

"That's it?"

"That's it, but it changed my life. It's like the humanity that wraps around all the organs makes the difference," he said.

Then he wrapped his arm around me and smiled and I knew what he meant. I rested my head against his shoulder and looked out the window. And then I ducked really quickly and nearly hit my chin on the counter.

"What?" Jonas asked. He looked hurt.

"Not you—them. Look!" I pointed out the window. Her parents could have been easily mixed up with other people, but Stella's flamingo wrap meant it could have only been her.

"I'm sorry," Jonas said. "I should have remembered this place was close to the hospital. They must have let her out for the afternoon."

"It's okay, it's a coincidence," I said, peering above the counter.

"Obie, I don't think they can see us," Jonas said, sliding down to the floor next to me. "I think the light is reflecting off the window and would go into their eyes if they looked over here."

The three of them were sitting under a tree and eating their own ice creams, no sharing. Stella was doing a lot of talking and gesturing. Her mom was pointing up like she was trying to push the clouds higher in the sky. Malloy was sitting with his arms crossed against his chest. His dark hair looked matted, like he hadn't washed it in days.

Whenever anyone opened the door to the ice cream shop, we caught small pieces of the conversation Stella was having with her parents. As the parlor door closed behind one customer, we heard Stella's mom say "—not wrong to rectify what's wrong in the world." Her voice was high pitched and preachy.

Another customer opened the door to leave after giving Jonas and me, crouched in front of our seats, an odd look. This time all I could hear were pieces of Stella's words. ". . . but you're [mumble mumble] and killing others [mumble]." Her voice, eyes, and hands reached upwards. My skin prickled. Mrs. Stein had done that all the time, but I didn't recognize it until I saw it in Stella. Jonas rubbed my forearm. Probably for two to three seconds.

The customer who'd come in earlier left, again looking at us on the floor, shrugging his shoulders and opening the door, careful not to drop his two cones.

"—who cares?" Stella was whining. "[mumble] not like we're modifying [mumbled] human . . ." She turned towards the parlor, and we got a clear snatch of the conversation. "—only repairing it along God's outline using organ printing. It's the original code, not a new one." She stomped her foot and Stella's mom shook her head abruptly.

Jonas leaned forward with his hands in prayer position and his thumbs pressed against his lips. His eyes darted to Stella's mom and back to Stella like watching a tennis match. We couldn't hear them anymore, but my heart was beating quickly just from watching. Then Stella made a gesture I was sure I'd made many times—shoulders hunched, elbows bent, palms facing up. It could only mean, *Why not?*

"BECAUSE IT VIOLATES GOD!"

We heard Malloy even though the door was closed, and he was facing the other way. Everyone around us looked up and out the window. I saw Stella's mouth turn down at the corners. The pink in her mom's cheeks kind of spread out in all directions and then turned a really interesting shade of purple. Then they all started walking back towards the hospital. Maybe the winds changed because I caught one more quiet sentence that Stella whispered.

"I have too much hindsight," she said, probably to herself.

Once they were gone and people turned back to their sweets, Jonas and I rose silently.

"What a weird position to be in—old and young at the same time," I said.

Jonas only gazed at his feet, fingering the tiny vial on his necklace.

Chapter 29

I told my parents about seeing Stella and her parents and everything I thought I'd heard. Being open seemed like a good idea at that point. Also, I knew I needed help and didn't even know what kind or how I'd get it.

"Look, Stella's in a tough spot," my mom empathized. "On one hand she's your age, on the other she has the grief and memories of a hundred-and-twenty-year-old woman in her head. Also, she's got a lot of guilt. I mean, she helped arrange a mass shooting where people were killed. And to top it off, it sounds more and more like she's thinking of her parents as criminals."

"Your mom and I have been talking a lot about Stella and the entire position we're in," my dad said, stroking the top of her head. "We feel pretty sorry for her in her current situation, and with those two parents of hers."

I nodded.

"It's also just very interesting to hear about her. I spent some time reading up on the brain." My dad brushed his hair

211

off his forehead. "We don't even know exactly where knowledge or memory is. Is it in brain cells in a certain area? Their molecules? The space between them?" he asked.

"I don't understand," I said.

"You introduced a memory into Stella—that cookie she was eating that she said she'd always loved. And she hadn't. Where did that come from? We don't know exactly."

"No . . . I just thought it was from the brain; I didn't think deeper than that."

My dad went on, "And you changed Stella. Like we were saying the other night, you implanted a set of ethics based on lessons and experience she never actually had. Now she's thinking of her parents' actions as a crime, not heroism."

My dad paused and gazed off, then snapped back. "Anyway, Obie, we wanted to talk to you about talking to Stella."

"Again?"

"Yes," my mom said, touching my hand. "I'd come with you too."

"We think it may be right to tell Stella what happened," my dad explained.

I stopped breathing for a moment. "What?!"

"Obie . . ." my mom started.

"But then she could turn me in! And . . . and . . ." *It's just too scary*, I thought.

"We think that she may turn her parents in," my dad said. "That would be the safest outcome here. The surgery you performed, the illegal spleen—everything would probably stay quiet, and the threat of her parents would go away."

Well, that would be nice.

My dad continued. "If they did talk, I think they'd have to admit to more crimes, like threatening you, and they'd never do that. Also, how would they ever prove anything you did wrong?"

"Also, Obie," my mom went on, "how did you feel about what that lab scientist Penn told you—that you had some of his DNA in your heart?"

I had trouble putting words to the weird twist in my stomach that Penn's news had given me. "Um, surprised? Well, shocked."

"So were we when you told us. It's like we have a new relative we didn't know about. And we would have liked to have known at the time what was about to happen," my mom said. I'd never thought about what that part of the story was like for them when I'd told it.

"Now think of Stella," my dad added. "She has an entire part of another person's mind inside her own and could live with that confusion for the rest of her life and never know why—in addition to all the other crap she's experiencing."

"But I could get into serious trouble," I said, hating myself for sounding selfish; but come on, we could just be quiet and maybe get away with everything if we could find a way to handle her parents.

"We've been talking about that," my dad said, "and have broken this down into a few scenarios."

I meant to groan inwardly but think some of it escaped my mouth, which my dad ignored as he rose and placed his hands behind his back.

"Scenario one is that Stella doesn't believe you, in which case you tried your best and can do no more." House lowered a drawing board even though I thought my mom and I had requested no encouragement of these lectures. My dad extended his finger to the board and drew a number two as he went on. "Scenario two is that she does believe you, and gets angry, and then reports you. In that case we could assume a defensive posture of feigned ignorance."

"A what?" my mom and I asked, even though I was pretty sure she'd already talked all this through with him.

"Who is going to believe that a—forgive me—fifteen-year-old girl performed a brain transplant? I mean, really? And especially when the story comes from the mouth of a person with severe brain damage."

I considered this and then nodded. "What's the next scenario?"

"Scenario three is that Stella not only believes you but empathizes with you. This is a muscle she seems to have been honing following her surgery based upon her comments on the shooting, her consideration of how bad it is to hurt others outside of self-defense, and her self-initiated question of whether to turn in her parents. Also, as we said, she literally has some of Mrs. Stein in her now, although we don't know exactly how much versus Stella's old self." He wrote this last point on the board and then labeled it with a question mark, which House changed into "Unknown Factor."

"So, then what? I tell her and she believes me and then what?" I asked.

"Then, she can move on and live her life knowing why she is the way she is. Or," he stood up straighter, "she can become very angry. She could become *incensed*."

"Incensed?"

"Imagine how mad you'd feel knowing that your parents not only conditioned you to help with a mass shooting," he explained, "but that the fear they ingrained in you made you fall off a bridge, and that they also threatened your childhood friend and her family and her friends? That they actually were going to hurt another person in your name?"

"Yeah," I said. When he put it that way, I could see how Stella could feel. "I'd be fuming mad. I'd feel like I had no power at all, and I'd get really angry at them."

"Would you turn them in?" my mom asked.

"Probably," I answered, pretty easily. "I'd do it to take charge of my life. Oh, and to keep them away from me for good." Then I suddenly felt heavy, as if my shoulders were being pressed down by weights.

"Obie, don't look so sad," my mom said.

"It's just a lot. Of decisions. And all at once," I told her.

"You were pulled into something, and you reacted as you needed to feel safe," she reassured me, putting her arm around me.

"Yes, but," my dad started. "Obie, I understand why you did what you did, but let's not act as if it was totally all right. If we were to have to go through all this again, I would not want you to touch that girl's brain."

I felt my stomach constrict with guilt. "No, I probably wouldn't do it again anyway."

"When we operated on Mrs. Stein's eye," my mom said, "we had a doctor, a nurse, and a robot. Plus Mrs. Stein was involved because she gave her consent for the procedure."

"I know, I know."

"Doing that surgery actually went against your name. Honey, you know the meaning of your name, right?" my mom asked.

"Yes, it means to obey God, but I always thought you just thought it sounded cute."

My dad chimed in. "Ah, well I do think it is cute, but we had more to go on than just that. We knew that your first moments in this world would involve a heart printing and transplant that would not have been possible fifty years ago. We knew you were going to grow up in a world of many, many choices and possibilities around life and health." He paused to clear his throat. I thought he seemed a little emotional. "The moments during your surgery when we waited, knowing our tiny baby was suffering, even if it was for the sake of her health, were very difficult for us and we wondered if we'd made the right decision for you. So, we thought, let's symbolically take some future burden off your shoulders by choosing the name, 'Obie.'"

"I don't understand."

"We liked 'obey God' because it indirectly meant don't be God," my mom explained. "We didn't know if you would ever choose to believe in a higher power, but we wanted to make sure you didn't have too much of a burden on your shoulders."

I thought for a few moments. "I didn't think that everything could get so complicated all of a sudden," I said. "I thought we were treating Stella for a hole in her brain, not changing her as a person. Not changing her entire family."

"Hey," my dad said. "Remember what the Rabbi said at Mrs. Stein's funeral? Sharing stories promotes kindness. Stella now shares Mrs. Stein's and has become kinder."

That was true. I felt some relief as his words integrated with my mind.

Then my dad added the line that I never forgot and that I chose to carry with me forever in those intricate molecules and cells in my head, and all the spaces between them.

"Obie, I want you to know how proud we are of you. You have tilted the world towards the positive."

And then I knew what I would do.

Chapter 30

I visited Stella at the hospital during a time when she said she'd be alone. My mom stood outside the door, and I was glad to know she was right there because I was sweaty and nervous. The first thing I noticed when I entered the room was that the stuffed animals that had been on Stella's bed were lying all over the floor. I tripped over a puffy blue kitten that made a squeaking noise as I moved into the chair next to Stella's bed.

"How've you been?" I asked.

"Well, I've lost my mind, but the doctors are helping," she sneered. She was sitting straight up in bed. Her flamingo wrap was crookedly placed around her head, and she chewed on one loose end as if it were a piece of candy.

"How do you mean?"

Stella tapped her comm and projected the screen onto the wall. "Look at my music recognition feed."

I had trouble reading the first word aloud. "Tum-bala-laika?"

"Yes. Do you know what that is?"

"No idea."

Stella tapped it. A melody I'd never heard began playing and a pop-up explanation said, "A Jewish folk song in the Yiddish language."

"I don't understand," I said.

"You don't? Imagine if you kept hearing it playing in your mind. Over and over until you had the words memorized—the Yiddish words, an ancient Jewish language you don't even speak. You know them so well you can even sing them into your comm and ask what it is. Imagine learning it was an actual song that has no business being in your head whatsoever. Like, none, zero, and it's just appeared and keeps playing at random times, when you're eating or peeing or walking down the hallway."

"Wow."

"Wow? That's all?" She stopped chewing on her cloth wrap and looked at me.

"Wow and I'm sorry? Sorry that you had to experience that . . . I mean, it's still pretty good not having a hole in your head. At least it was filled with music and not, um . . ."

"What? Porn?"

"That wasn't what I'd been thinking but sure." Actually, it was exactly what I'd been thinking.

"I told the doctors about it—hearing a song play randomly—and that's why they're keeping me in the hospital for longer. They treated me for a mild stroke and the music turned off. Now I'm just waiting to see if there's another . . . broadcast."

219

I probably deserved a prize for not giggling right then. Instead, I inhaled and told her the truth of why she was hearing that song.

"I may be able to explain," I started. I didn't begin the story with Stella's parents' role because I thought it would be too harsh of an opening. *It's the craziest thing. Did you know your parents threatened me?* Instead, I started with the fall from the bridge. Stella listened quietly the entire time I spoke except for when I described how I'd removed the casing from her skull and put Mrs. Stein's brain inside. Then she flinched, sucked in her breath, and blinked a few times but didn't laugh or cry. When I was done, she remained still, looking at me silently. I thought I may have stunned or overwhelmed her and should have waited to have this conversation until she'd fully recovered and gone back home, but then I'd have to face her parents again.

When she did finally speak, she had a question.

"Who. Is. The. Girl?" she asked, leaning forward more and more with each word, her cheeks flushing as she gazed at me.

"Girl?"

"The one who I dream about, like I told you. It's always her, the same girl with the bright blue eyes and the face shaped like an oval. She's gotta be someone specific. And I'm always sad to see her but I don't want the dream to end."

"Um."

"Obie," Stella's voice quivered, "just tell me."

"That's probably Nava, Mrs. Stein's daughter. She died of a heart defect over eighty years ago."

"Why does she carry a list of names?"

"A list of names? I really don't know."

"Come on, give me something, Obie. I'm going crazy here," she looked at me with her eyes narrowed. "Or maybe you inserted someone else's crazy into me," she added, her voice getting higher and louder.

"Tell me something else about the list." I was hoping to buy some time. I didn't really think I could help, and I was trying to remember all the scenarios my dad had reviewed. What was supposed to happen if Stella got angry again? I wiped my palms on my pants.

"It says 1953 on top," she said. "I think there are that many names on the list."

Then it clicked. "Oh, now it makes sense; it's the year 1953. That's when Mrs. Stein's grandfather went to Israel to look for his brother."

"Why?"

"Because of the Holocaust. Mrs. Stein was Jewish and so was her family, and they were all split up during the second world war. She had a copy of the missing person forms her grandfather filled out in 1953 framed in her home."

"Did he find his brother?"

"No," I shook my head. "No, he died, or was killed, I suppose I should say." I looked at her, this time with my eyes narrowed. "They were labeled undesirable; they were hated for what they were, and then they were exterminated."

Stella leaned forward. "Why did you do this to me? Why did you give me this history and this . . . this burden?" Her voice was low and trembled with anger.

"Because your parents said they were going to kill me. Your mom told me that if you didn't get better, my parents would know what it was to lose what they love. Your dad even broke into my House and left a poster of your damaged brain on my bedroom ceiling," I told her. I'd been planning to say it gently, but it came out like a harsh whisper. I showed her a photo of the poster Malloy had left behind.

"What?" She leaned back in her bed.

"And I didn't even do anything," I told her, trying not to sound whiny. "All I did was want to live and to help Mateo after you guys had him shot." My breath came out so quickly that the word "shot" kind of sounded like an actual bullet being fired. Stella started to cry then, and I felt sorry for her.

"You would have really liked Mrs. Stein," I went on. "She was amazing. She valued life. She lost all this family in war and then she lost her own daughter because she wasn't born at a time where she could get the kind of help that I did. And did she stop living? Or become angry and mean? No!" I pounded my fists against my legs. "She decided that her ancestors' good deeds and their religion and beliefs and everything would continue through her!" I stopped because I realized I was making Stella's parents sound like evil infammards by comparison, which they actually were even without comparison.

Stella pressed her palms against her eyes, but her tears flowed past them and down her cheeks. "My parents told me that everything we did was for the good of society." Her shoulders shook with sobs. I sat there squeezing my palms together, wondering if I should bring my mother in or if that could make this worse. Look at my own mom; she heals people for a living, and she's never asked me to hurt anyone!

"It's even worse than I thought," Stella wept.

"Worse?"

"My parents . . . they said that science was making everything into a weapon."

"I don't understand," I said.

"The way you hijacked that surgical robot and you attacked me," she explained.

Whoa.

"And your printed heart made you into a weapon too," she added.

Double whoa. I stared at Stella, wondering if it was actually impossible to change someone's mind (without a full brain transplant) or if everything I said or did would just be turned around and used against me because of her perspective. Then I remembered two things. Stella had seemed doubtful about whether her parents did the right thing when Jonas and I eavesdropped on her from the ice cream parlor, and she was literally facing her parents' murderous actions right now. Who'd want to deal with a thing like that? My next sentence was going to be crucial. It needed to show Stella what my dad would call "my position," and be sensitive enough to not make her hate me more.

Obie's Rapid-Fire Mental Calculations

Dad would say: Don't do it until you know what it is. Don't make a move until you know the direction.

Output: Remain silent now. Think.

Mom would say: Remember that everyone has their perspective and that people in hospitals are often speaking from pain. The pain is always real.

Output: Recognize Stella's pain when you speak.

House would say: There are illogical statements in this conversation when reflected against the overall situation.

Output: Point out the contradiction. Gently.

"Stella," I began, keeping my tone as calm and steady as I could even though she'd just called me a weapon, "I understand that no one wants to face, uh . . . (*too strong—abort word!*) . . . to turn around and see evil . . . (*insert additional word to avoid calling a whole person evil*) . . . deeds being done around them, especially by their family. But science didn't hijack the guns at the volunteer event and make them shoot innocent people. I suppose science made it possible, but it didn't actually do it (*leave out who did in hopes Stella will reach this conclusion. Now stop talking*)."

"No," Stella agreed, staring at her palms. "My parents did that." She sounded as if she'd lost her voice screaming at a concert.

All right. What was I supposed to say now? Maybe you could turn your parents in, so they have a small chance of getting out of prison reformed and not killing people anymore?

"Obie . . ." she looked at me, her red-rimmed eyes wide and desperate. "I don't know how I can believe in goodness, or in morality, or even in God if there is so much evil out there. I mean, I have to sit in a hospital bed with another person's brain inside my own because my own parents threatened you because of what is keeping you alive." *Whoa*. "Not that I think you did the right thing," she glared at me, then went on. "And I have to feel the misery of a woman whose daughter died. And she even lost family in the Holocaust, which I am going to have to read more about later, but I already know that a lot of that came from hatred like my parents threatened you with." *Again whoa*.

Obie's Even More Rapidly Fired Mental Calculations
Mrs. Stein would say . . .?

She was dead, so she'd really say nothing.

What could I say to honor her?

Her mind was inside me too but in a different way—through her friendship and mentoring.

I inhaled deeply, and when I answered Stella, I spoke for both of us.

"Goodness is found in the midst of evil, Stella. It's found in your response to it."

Chapter 31

Now I'd done the right thing and could just wait. Maybe Stella would turn in her parents. Or maybe we could just say we'd tried and make another plan in case her parents came after us once they realized their daughter was no longer their favorite pet.

And wait I did, but not in the way I'd thought that I would. I didn't hear from Jonas for two days. Two long days. On the first, I assumed he didn't want to come on too strong. Good. Too much at once would be bad, right? Clearly this was all part of his strategy.

On the second day I checked his social feeds about every fifteen minutes. They were empty. Okay, maybe he'd decided to withdraw and reflect for a bit on our shared experiences. That's why I waited until morning on the third day to send him the word "Wassuup?" after about twenty minutes of looking up slang from the year 2020. He didn't reply.

I fretted over if I'd done or said anything wrong. I reread my old messages to see what I could have misinterpreted or mis-stated. I mentally plotted a timeline of major events between our meeting and today. I could see no issues. So, I happened to plan to walk and then happened to actually walk by Jonas' store. It was closed. I peeked in the windows, making sure Jonas' body wasn't lying on the floor anywhere inside. If he'd fallen off a ladder and died, that would explain why he hadn't contacted me. I mean, that would be the best explanation even in a twisted way. But the store was empty. I went by the ice cream shop, and he wasn't there either. It was filled with kids laughing and fighting and smearing their faces with chocolate.

My feet took me to the hospital. I think my legs went onto autopilot while I wondered what was going on. Maybe my subconscious thought that I could avoid obsessing over Jonas by taking in nature and strolling outside the garden I'd run through the day of the surgery. People were sitting on benches and enjoying the sunshine. I would have gone in and relaxed a bit, but I was still a little afraid that I'd be recognized somehow. I jumped pretty high when I heard my name.

"Obie?"

I nervously turned around. It was Penn, the lab scientist. It actually took me a moment to remember the man whose cardiac DNA I'd been gifted. So much had happened since he'd told me about that. He smiled. His teeth were in his mouth, and he was carrying what looked like a vanilla cone.

"Everything okay?" he asked. "Sorry to scare you."

"Everything's fine," I lied. I bet he could tell.

"I think I could show you something to cheer you up," he offered. "Can you come to the lab?"

I balked and tried to think of excuses. Upset stomach, another brain surgery, a homework assignment of digging a hole and lying in it.

"I think you want to see this, kiddo," Penn added.

"Okay," I mumbled and followed him inside the building. How could I say no to an invitation like that?

When we were inside, Penn took a seat by the surgical robot I'd used to dissect Mrs. Stein's brain. There was a brain in the flask on the tray. A familiar set up.

"Say hello to Sarah Stein," Penn said, pointing. "Or, to her leftovers."

I winced.

"Too soon for humor?" he asked. "Alright, I get it. I'm going to get right to the point." He punched a bunch of keys on the robot console, and I perched on a stool. Pretty soon the lights that had assessed the brain and all of its parts and their locations for me began to shine. "Notice anything unusual?" Penn asked.

I got up and walked over to the flask. The gray tissue was again reflecting colors against the glass container. I saw a blur move across the walls. It wasn't as clear as Nava's face had been, but it moved . . . intentionally.

"Well," I said, trying to sound scientific, "what's unusual is that the memory isn't as clear as it was when I was doing the dissection."

"So, you've seen this type of thing before? Okay," Penn said. "You're lucky. So far scientists have only had anecdotal reports of what we call memory signaling. But check this out." He typed a few commands and the lights moved. They shone deep inside the cut, into where it looked like a slice of cake had been taken out. Gross, but that's probably the best way to explain it.

Then a little girl's reflection appeared on the glass. I leaned closer. The girl was not the same shape as Nava had been in the running image I'd seen of her. Her legs were thinner and her hair longer. She felt familiar. She was playing on a surface, maybe lying on the floor. Then she turned and looked in my direction and I realized that I was seeing myself.

It was like watching a video of my childhood through a grainy and old-fashioned lens setting. I watched my child self open her mouth, to laugh, I think—but of course there was no sound. Then the child rolled onto her back and stretched her tiny arms.

"Oh my," I said, my mouth open and dry.

"I thought it was you," Penn said. "Pretty neat, huh?"

"I don't know what to say."

"Describe what you see," he instructed.

"I'm looking at myself through another person's eyes. I'm young and I look happy and…" What was the word? "I don't know what else. There's something else."

"Is it good or bad?" Penn asked.

"Good," I answered. *But how so?* I was watching myself from afar and as objectively as I ever had, like a character on a TV show. It was like looking at a world in itself somehow. And then I knew what the right word was. "It's whole," I explained. "I look whole, like all of me is there and it's all fine."

I looked over at Penn and saw him smiling. "What a gift Sarah was," he said. "She just keeps giving."

"Why does this reflection thing happen with her brain?" I asked.

"Again, we've only got anecdotes from the scientific community," he said. "But I've got a theory. It's that this happens with people who live their lives consciously."

"I don't understand."

"In short, her memories are clear because her vision was."

"But, um . . ." I wasn't sure how to ask this next question without sounding self-absorbed.

"Why you?" he suggested.

"Yes."

"I think you meant a great deal to her. I can't think of any other reason," he said.

Was that supposed to make me feel better? The perspective of seeing myself as Mrs. Stein's memory was lovely; I mean, it was a nice reminder that my life was . . . okay and intact, if that was the right description. But then I started to miss her so much, and to wonder when life had become so complicated. What would Mrs. Stein have said about Jonas? And when had I stopped feeling the natural confidence of childhood? The younger me wouldn't have cared as much about him as I did now.

"You've given me a lot to think about," I said. But the truth was I didn't want to think about anything. I'd borrowed that line from my dad. He used it when he wanted to get out of a work meeting early. I thanked Penn for showing the memory to me and walked out.

I thought I'd pass by the garden again on my way home. It was nice to take in the scenery from a distance—kids visiting elderly patients, people throwing frisbees, Jonas sitting next to Stella on a bench. *What?*

I stopped abruptly and the woman behind me walked right into me.

"Sorry, I um, sorry," I mumbled to her, then looked back to make sure I was right. Yes, Jonas was sitting next to Stella. Her head was wrapped in that stupid flamingo cloth, and his body was turned to face her with his arm resting on the backrest. He was leaning forward like an eager little boy or a newborn puppy near its mother. I couldn't move. I was stuck between the anxieties of being seen and of learning what was going on over there on the bench. Maybe it would be better not to know? But I had to know.

I ambled over in their direction, making sure to admire all the flowers and pulling my hair to cover the side of my face. I could just hear their conversation. I crouched behind the tall flowers that had smacked Jonas in the face and pretended to inspect each individual purple petal.

"But you did so much," Stella was saying. "As much as you could at the time. That is all that anyone can do."

"I feel so useless," Jonas said. I didn't know how anyone like Jonas could feel like that, unless it came to messaging me back, then he was definitely useless. "It's like I could always do more."

"That will prevent you from actually doing more, from using your inner strength," she replied. *What the heck am I hearing?* I wondered, craning my neck to get a better view. "You did as much as you could and of what you could control," Stella said. It looked like she put her hand on his. My stomach twisted. I performed brain surgery. All she did was say pretty things.

"But it wasn't enough, that's exactly the point," Jonas replied, shaking his head.

"No, the point is that there is more to life than saving it. There is also love, and I can tell you did, and you do. And I know what that means now. It means everything."

Wait, did Jonas just tell Stella that organ printing wasn't enough? Or that I wasn't enough?

"Jonas, you know that feeling guilty doesn't mean that you are guilty," Stella added.

Did he feel guilty over abandoning me? Was she taking him from me?

"Don't undermine what you were able to provide. It was significant," she continued. "And with your other work, it's as if you are saving the world over and over. And I'm not just saying that to make you feel better," she wrapped up.

So, I was significant to him and I'm supposed to be happy with that and move on? Couldn't he at least have told me?

Jonas either became silent or too quiet for me to hear. I pushed the flower stems apart and tried to get a good look. He was gazing at his feet, fingering the tiny vial on his necklace as Stella uttered muffled words that sounded like "you were your brother's keeper . . . save a life … like saving the world." Then Jonas looked up and right in my direction. I ducked my head and rushed out of that garden for the second time. I felt like a fool. I'd been at home thinking about Jonas, ready to talk about anything, big or small, and here he was pouring his heart out to Stella. I wondered if he realized that her average

age was sixty-seven and a half. Was that what drew him to her? Or maybe he ignored it because she was pretty, even pretty enough to ignore her murderous family.

"Sorry, Obie," Mateo said. I'd caught him on his deck again. He was using old utensils to build a tower for a vine to climb on as it grew.

"Do you think I could use that EmpathSpin thing to see what Jonas is doing?"

"No, I do not," Mateo answered, pausing his work, fork in hand. "You need to communicate the old-fashioned way."

"What's that?"

"Talking."

"Oh. But he didn't reply to my message."

"Then let the guy come to you," Mateo said. "Don't chase him."

"I wonder what he saw when he looked at me and when he looked at Stella, like, what his memories will be."

"Who cares what he thinks of Stella?" Mateo added a baby spoon to his tower.

"It's just . . . well . . ."

"Spit it out," he said.

"I guess I feel like my creation is outshining me, okay?" Mateo dropped a fork and looked up at me.

"I know it's wrong," I added. "I just can't help it."

"What's wrong with it is that you think you own Stella now," he said.

"I don't think I own her, I just . . . I don't know."

"You think she owes you something," Mateo suggested, crossing his arms over his chest and nodding.

"Yeah."

"Obie, *amiga*, the problem you solved by tinkering with her brain was the one where her parents were threatening us. You didn't solve *her*."

"But she woke up with a better sense of right and wrong."

"Yes, she did, but you don't get to say what is right or wrong with her, or what needed fixing."

"Huh? But it's wrong what she did. She helped the shooting," I protested.

"Yes, and I'm very glad the law agrees with you because otherwise we'd be ruined. But you and I don't get to decide this for other people. When they hurt us, we get to stop them, but we don't get to reach into their minds and change who they are as people."

"Why the heck not?"

"Because it's too powerful. Look, every time someone throws trash at my head when I'm walking down the street or calls me a machine, it pisses me off, okay? But I don't want to create a society that can turn against me even more."

"How would society turn against you more?" I didn't get it. If I could fix Stella's problems, why shouldn't I?

"Because Stella had a point about science making weapons. She just didn't understand that everything we make these days is both good and bad, self-defense and offense, because it depends on how you use it and how people react. The same stuff that made my eye work also made me a target. That's my life, and that's it." He paused to select three table

234

knives with grapes engraved on the handles. He turned on a blowtorch and applied a thin stream of heat to them. "You opened the door to probing people's brains and memories, Obie. That has serious mad scientist potential."

"Eh?"

"Think if it this way. What if I could identify a specific memory in one person, take it out, and put it into someone else, like you did?"

I considered this. "I guess you could really change people, even if they didn't want to be changed."

"Right," Mateo said, turning off the blowtorch. "If we can transplant memories, we could also replace people's values. You think if Mrs. Stein didn't have all that Holocaust trauma in her family she'd be as . . . as tolerant of others who were unlike her, but peaceful? You think I would be as accepting of others if I didn't know what it was like to be treated like the muck of society?"

It hurt to hear Mateo call himself that.

"I suppose not," I answered. "It is possible you wouldn't be, although it's really up to you how to react to that."

"That's not my point," Mateo said, bending the soft metal of the knives and twisting them a bit. "My point is that, if memories shape our values and who we are as people, wouldn't implanting them also mean that we could be assigning an idea of good and bad when we did the transplantation?"

"Yeah, works for me." I tried to make a joke. He didn't laugh.

"But who gets to decide what is good and what is bad? I'm undesirable today—"

"Mateo you are very desirable—"

"You know what I mean, Obie. What I'm saying is what if one day society decided that those Humanists were more desirable and should be implanted into others?"

"That would suck."

"Yes, it would. And that's why brain transplants are illegal. I'm sure of it," Mateo twisted the now soft knives around each other in a pattern. I realized he was braiding them. "Look at Mrs. Stein and the Holocaust again. Yes, it was wrong, it was evil, it was bad. But so many of those bad guys thought they were doing good! The same way people who throw crap at me think they are doing the world a favor. And so, our Public Policy AI system decided that messing with the brain was off limits. Maybe it knew that societies can change, or be trendy." He finished his table knife braid. "So, the AI said, no way, there was going to be a point where science would have to stop. It took power out of our hands so it wouldn't be in anyone's."

Mateo held up the braid. I could no longer tell it had been made with knives. The sun gleamed off the silver. "See, Obie; what a tool does, whether it is good or bad, really depends on whose hands it's in. And that's why we need laws, or bibles— or whatever you want to call the moral code—to save us from ourselves."

He bent over and inserted the braid above the climbing vine, then pulled the leaves around it. It was beautiful.

"Now I feel bad about what I did," I said. It was true, this was all very heavy.

"Don't feel bad, Obie," he said. "It turned out okay, and you were under fire. But don't get self-righteous either."

I nodded. "I'm going to go home for dinner," I said, standing. I needed a break.

"Okay," he said. "And one more thing. If Jonas prefers Stella to you that means they can have each other, okay? You deserve more."

Gosh I have a good friend.

Chapter 32

The next morning, I had House project an exercise routine video onto the wall. Stretch up, down, lean side, lean side. Who needed more than this? Life would clearly move forward on smooth rails. I could calm down from performing an illegal brain operation, finding love, reaching the brink of changing humanity, and then losing love! I caught myself spacing out and standing still, then increased the volume on the video and got back into it. STRETCH UP, DOWN, LEAN SIDE, LEAN SIDE!

Then my comm buzzed with a message. I wasn't going to read it. I was going to let it wait for at least an hour. I was exercising! I didn't want to be interrupted.

Five seconds later I was staring at my comm. The message wasn't from Jonas. It was from Stella, and it was pretty disturbing:

Obie, my grief is winning. My daughter speaks to me at night and asks why her death makes no sense when others are killed for living in a way that she could not. I must take action. I cannot live another way.

I forwarded the message to Jonas and Mateo with emergency status. I didn't know what else to do. My mom was visiting patients and my dad was giving a lecture. We had been a team once, hadn't we?

They both replied immediately.

"Uh-oh," Mateo wrote.

"Her grief is winning?" Jonas wrote.

"Is she going to hurt herself?" Mateo asked.

"Meet at the hospital ASAP," Jonas replied. "I'll contact them on my way."

I was a bit ashamed that my first thought was, *So, Stella might be in trouble and Jonas replies ASAP?* Also, that my next action was to change my shirt really quickly, just to not be in a sweaty one.

But then I ran, getting to the speed rail as quickly as I could and then to the hospital. I relied on my heart once again to enter the building and to keep me calm as I sprinted down the hallways. They have monitors to stop self-harm, right? They must. Haven't we figured out a way to protect people from themselves by now?

Door after door unlocked in front of me, each just a few seconds after my imagination had conjured an image of Stella lying on the floor on the other side, bleeding from a self-inflicted wound or moaning and clutching her stomach. Behind each entrance point only stretched more hallway.

Was this my fault? Why didn't my dad mention this scenario? Why did I follow his advice and confront Stella about her parents?

It was the longest run of my life. When I reached Stella's door, I threw it open and stood there breathless. She was lying in bed. Her parents were sitting on either side. They looked at me, their eyes wide with wonder and then narrow with anger. I could not speak. I could only brace my hands against my skinny knees and pant. Then I felt a warm hand rub my back between my shoulder blades and turned around. It was Jonas, with Mateo a few paces behind him. Why was Jonas being affectionate with me?

"What are you doing here?" Stella's mom asked. Malloy moved to perch on the foot of Stella's bed and looked at me the way people look at each other to ask if a chair is taken—supposedly innocent and friendly but please don't say no because I will break you. I avoided eye contact with him. *I know you are bad,* I thought. *Don't play coy with me.*

I didn't answer.

"Well, this was a good visit," her mom announced. "Thanks for coming by."

"Not yet, Mom," Stella said.

"Stella seems less obedient," Mateo whispered to me. "I hope it doesn't wear off like the anesthesia."

Jonas didn't speak and kept his gaze fixed on Malloy. At least he wasn't looking at Stella.

"I'm actually glad they're here. Mateo, I wanted to talk to you," she said.

"To me?" he asked, looking behind him as if there were another Mateo standing there.

"Yes. Please sit down. I have to ask you something."

Mateo shuffled over to an empty chair and sat timidly on the edge. I don't think any of us knew what to expect.

Stella sat up a bit and cleared her throat. "I love my parents. I don't think I can ever not love them, even with what they've done. But I have this feeling within my skin now where I know what it is to lose a child, even though I haven't. And I feel ashamed of myself for the role I played in the shooting at your volunteer event."

I inhaled. Mateo's mouth opened in surprise and his eyes became watery.

"I am sorry, Mateo," she went on. "I am sorry for the pain you felt in your body from the bullet, in your soul from knowing hate, and in your family's life from coming so close to losing you. I have always believed in forgiveness, but that it must be earned, not just be given. That is both why I cannot forgive my parents for what they've done, and why I'm turning them in."

Mateo's crossed leg dropped, and his foot hit the floor loudly. Her mom emitted a short cry and buried her face in her hands. Stella ignored her and continued. "Mateo, will you forgive me for what I did to you? I would ask mercy from those who did not survive the shooting, but that chance will never be given to me; it is impossible. All I can do is ask for you to consider giving me yours and hope that maybe one day you will offer it to me."

Mateo closed his eyes. I wanted to go to him but sensed that I couldn't penetrate the cocoon he'd just woven around himself. I saw the invisible trauma of what he'd gone through swirling around his skin, not only the shooting but also the years of smiling in spite of people throwing their garbage at him, attacking him with their drones, avoiding him in the hallways, getting out of the swimming pool when he entered, and more insults and injuries than I probably knew about. He'd grinned without complaint as he cleaned trash and he'd insisted on living a life of integrity.

"Stella," he said, looking at her, his voice sturdy and clear. The red rim around his eyes made the blue one even bluer. "I forgive you."

"Thank you, Mateo," Stella said, "for giving me that. Because of you, I can still believe the world is good."

I wanted to enjoy the silence that followed, to let the closure hold me like a prolonged embrace. I wanted to preserve the gratitude that flowed through me for as long as possible, to notice all the details so I'd be able to recall them at any time for the rest of my life.

But then Malloy decided to interfere. I'd kind of forgotten he was there because of the conversation unfolding in front of me. The worst sorts of evil can do that—make you forget they're there until they show up in your home all of a sudden and scare you. Which he did; he really scared me.

First, he started cackling with his face upturned and his entire mouth open as if he expected to drink from the ceiling. Then he yelled at me. "What did you do to her?"

I felt my knees weaken in fear and my jaw tighten in anger.

"Dad, they didn't do anything, okay?" Stella answered. "You know that saying, 'Revenge is living well, without you'? Do that instead of fighting with them."

I knew that saying. Mrs. Stein taught it to me because she didn't want me to get caught up in this bad mess.

Malloy ignored his daughter. "I will get you, machines, for whatever you've done to her," he snarled.

Jonas stepped between us with his fists squeezed. I wondered why he was being protective of me, then I got distracted for a second because his biceps stood out pretty nicely. "Leave her alone," he growled.

Malloy pivoted towards Mateo and raised his fists against his second target. Stella and I started screaming.

"Don't touch him!" I shrieked.

"We'll do it together, the same way we've done everything until now!" her mom roared.

Mateo, my skinny little friend, faced his opponent, his arms up to block the pending blow. Jonas threw himself across Stella's bed to reach them. I grabbed Stella's mom's arm and yanked her back. She swiped at me with her other hand, and I heard something rip but I didn't know what. I didn't care to look. I was too afraid.

The panic in my stomach froze slowly in an outward ripple. I knew that only a moment was passing, but I could feel the fear move like rings growing in a tree. I was scared that Mateo would get hurt. I was scared that he'd be killed. I realized how horrible it would be for him to survive a shooting and then die like this. I wondered what I'd do without him. As the last ring grew, I thought about how full my life had been and how I didn't want it to change this way—didn't want to know the grief of losing a loved one like Mrs. Stein had known.

And then Stella's parents just halted. I mean, their bodies stopped moving and their mouths stopped working. Jonas, Mateo, and I looked at each other confusedly, then back at her parents who were still frozen. Jonas waved his hand in front of Malloy's face a few times and then Mateo actually tapped the man's cheek. It made a pretty amusing, hollow sound since Malloy's mouth was open. Only his astonished eyeballs moved in reaction.

Huh?

"Got 'em good," a voice said from the doorway. A police officer was standing there, a stun gun in her hand, her yellow painted nails glistening under the hospital lighting. I recognized her from the scene of Stella's accident.

"When I said I was turning my parents in," Stella said, "I meant now." She smiled meekly and looked teary. Her parents both hunched downward and groaned.

"When the stun starts wearing off, it always makes them lose slight control of their bowels," the officer said, smirking a little. Malloy tried to stand before giving up and lying in the fetal position on the floor. I felt relief thaw my insides.

Then Malloy ruined it again.

"You piece of crap robot kids," he said, his face pressed sideways against the floor. "This isn't going to go down like that at all. COMM—LAUNCH MALLOY-WARE ATTACK."

Malloy's comm vibrated loudly and started spewing rays of light.

Another attack? I grabbed Jonas' arm and squeezed it so hard he'd probably need new bones later. We crouched and braced ourselves.

"How did . . .? I don't understand . . ." Malloy stammered. We looked up. His comm had projected bright images against the front wall, displaying ten tiny squares showing retinal scans. I could see all these different pink and red blood vessel patterns depicted in circular photos. Each one had the logo of a sheriff's badge in the lower right corner. "What the heck?" both Malloy and the police officer exclaimed at the same time.

"Not much of a cyberattack," Jonas observed, putting his arm around me and making me feel even more confused than I knew possible.

"Those are the retinal scans of the entire Law Enforcement Civilian Protection Squad," the officer said in horrified wonder. "The ones guarding the volunteers at the beach cleanup and the rest of the group. You criminal hacker. That's how you got them to shoot at those poor people."

Malloy turned to me. "You did this somehow," he said. "You, I will—"

"You will do nothing," the officer said, grabbing his wrists. As she handcuffed both of Stella's parents, her mom started crying silently, her mouth working but unable to form words. Malloy just stared at the ground, his lips pursed, and his shoulders hunched.

They silently looked at their daughter before they were taken down the hall. Stella looked back, her hands resting in her lap, her bright eyes observant. I felt nothing when I saw this. Maybe my heart was immune to their pain by then, or maybe the whole experience was too much and I was just done.

Stella faced me silently for a moment. I thought she was going to say something profound. Instead, she said, "Obie, your shirt is torn."

She was right—that must have been the tearing sound I'd heard while we were all fighting. It went right down the middle of the top half of my shirt and revealed my camisole. The scar on my breastbone was clearly visible. I did not care. Not even a little. Let Stella remember me this way forever, just let her.

Chapter 33

"What do you mean you're mad at me?" Jonas asked. We were in the garden, a place I never wanted to visit again after this. Mateo had gone home to tell his family the news.

"You disappeared."

"I, uh, had some things to take care of," he said, shrugging and looking down.

"Like new friendships to forge?" I asked. I was too exhausted to be polite. Maybe my brain was now a hundred and twenty years old. There was no holding back.

Jonas looked me in the eye and squinted. "I guess Stella told you?"

I didn't answer. I wasn't about to admit I'd spied on him.

"Obie, she's been helping me with some things," Jonas said.

"Things?"

"Yeah." He stuffed his hands into his pockets. If he'd reached lower, he could have fit his fingers into the stupid holes in his vintage jeans. Wasn't he cold? He cleared his

247

throat. "Things with my mom. I've always felt like I should have saved her, and I didn't."

Eh? That was not what I'd been expecting to hear.

"I don't understand."

"Well, Stella mentioned this line about being your brother's keeper?" He looked at me as if to ask if I knew of it. I didn't. "It has to do with being responsible for others."

"But you already seem to feel responsible. And guilty." What I'd overheard was starting to make sense in this new light.

"Right, but Stella also pointed out that I did live up to my responsibility. She said that it was like medicine for a mother to see her child who loved her and spent time at her bedside. And it was all that I could have done for her anyway." I'd never thought of Jonas as in need of . . . anything. Especially not reassurance. This was fascinating. And a bit sad. I looked at him shuffling his feet around in the dirt.

"Why didn't you tell me?" I asked.

"I felt sort of embarrassed. I mean, you implanted a brain, Obie."

Wait, I intimidated him?! Mateo had been right. I started laughing. "Jonas," I stuttered, "I'm, I'm not laughing at you."

"Really because it looks like you totally are," he said, unsmiling.

"No! No. I am laughing at this situation. You getting some advice from Mrs. Stein, in a way. It's weird. What a weird life we're living." And, as much as this was a cover for what I'd just realized—that I was the intimidating one—this was true, just perhaps not the whole truth behind my giggles. "But you should have told me at least something, Jonas."

He nodded. "I'm sorry."

"It's okay," I said, wondering if I should pat his shoulder and deciding it would be too awkward. "I understand now. And I also think you did the right thing for your mom. You did all that you could." We stood there quietly for a moment. "Really, she was so lucky to have you," I added. "I mean, I put my parents through hell with all this transplant stuff. You get the 'good child' medal if there is one."

Jonas laughed. "Want to visit me tomorrow?" he asked. "We can have lunch." Then he put his hand on my shoulder. It wasn't awkward at all.

I was going to hold back but he looked so sad standing there with the daylight starting to fade and his thin "This is A Costume" t-shirt the only thing keeping him warm.

"Sure," I said. I was still mad that he'd disappeared on me but felt much better now that I understood he'd been seeking help and was too self-conscious to show me that side of him. Maybe things could work out now. Maybe it would all be okay.

"Obie, why aren't you asleep?" House asked. "Your enemies are in jail. Your friends are alive and well. Your pulse oximetry shows general relaxation prior to sleep."

"Too much. Just too much." Even though the Jonas question had been answered I couldn't relax.

"Is there an unresolved issue that is at the forefront or in the background of your mind?"

I slowly reviewed the day in reverse order, starting with my parents' reaction when I told them Stella had turned in her parents. It was ecstatic. My dad had applauded, and my mom had squeezed me tightly. House had served Korean rice pancakes for dinner. And then my parents said I could go back to in-person school, which I missed even though it was old-fashioned.

When I went over the visit with Stella in my mind, I thought of one question. "I don't understand why Malloy's comm spewed out those retinal scans when he tried to launch whatever cyberattack he had in mind," I told House.

Silence.

"House? Is there a follow-up question?"

"The configuration of Malloy's comm was sufficiently unique for recognition as the origin of Obie Real-Time Location System Breach."

"Eh?"

Silence.

"House, what are you not telling me?"

"After the location-tracking portion of your comm was hacked, I felt very bad according to my programming. When Malloy entered our physical home, guised as a repairman, I recognized him as the originator of the hack. I then duplicated myself, and when he tried to leave behind malware, I allowed him to do so inside of the decoy."

"But why would his comm spew evidence of his crimes?"

"In exchange for the malware, my duplicate sent him something as well at the exact same time when the channel was open. You could say that it paid him for his visit and left

250

a unique tip, maybe designed to deploy if he tried to harm you again."

House protected me?! Houses weren't allowed to commit crimes or hack . . . but having a duplicate probably helped.

"Where is your duplicate now?"

"Destroyed."

I felt myself relax and realized that I was less vulnerable with such a great team. My parents, Jonas and Mateo, and House.

"Thank you," I said. But I still couldn't sleep.

"What else?" House asked.

"What do you think is going to happen to Stella now?"

"I don't know."

My comm buzzed.

"U up?" Mateo messaged.

"Yea."

"Me too. Really nervous," he wrote.

"Y?"

"Starting work tomorrow."

"U didn't tell me you got a job?" I asked.

"My end of the bargain w/Jonas. I said I'd work in his store for a month on wknds & I got a spleen," he typed.

I realized I'd totally forgotten about the deal we'd made at Mateo's house over rugelach.

"BTW," Mateo added, "My dad said that Stella's parents turned in a bunch of other people in exchange for some kind of a deal. All organ printing centers are probably going to be able to lessen security now and just go back to business."

That was a relief. No one would have to go through what we'd gone through again. Maybe life could go back to normal, or at least imitate normalcy as much as possible. Mateo and I could go to school in peace.

"There's still one problem," Mateo wrote.

Crap. What did he need me to do now? Take Stella's brain out and put it into someone else?

"WHAT?" I asked.

"No idea what to wear to the store. I hate vintage threads."

Chapter 34

The next morning, I found my parents drinking coffee and looking happy but tired.

"What a wild ride we've all had!" my dad said when I sat down. I noticed he was eating rugelach for breakfast. A lot.

"What's going to happen to Stella now?" I asked.

"I made a few calls this morning," my mom told me. "Stella has an aunt who . . . well, it sounds like she received an artificial liver years ago and was ostracized by the family. She would like to take Stella in."

"That's good, I guess," I said.

"It is," my dad said.

My mom handed me a plate and we ate cookies for breakfast in silence, looking out the window at the pigeons.

Jonas messaged me, "Hope you slept well. Looking forward to seeing you today!" It made me feel warm. I went into my room to get ready. Long night or not, I was going to have lunch with Jonas and would get to see Mateo working in retail. Fun!

"I'm coming to see you!" I messaged him, and then noticed the icon of an unread holographic message blinking in the corner. I pressed it and Stella appeared in my room, pre-recorded, semi-transparent but life-like. She stood above the center of my bed, beneath where the poster of her brain had been hung. She wore regular clothing and was bald. She held a suitcase in one hand and looked uncertainly at what must have been the camera recording her. I moved over a bit so I could see her face better. Her expression was nervous, like a little girl going to school on the first day.

"Obie," she said, "I've been thinking things over. I do that a lot now. It's actually easier for me than looking forward. It's like my clock is running backwards and all I see is hindsight." She cleared her throat and looked down.

"I'm still pretty angry that you put stuff in my head. I mean, I get it, you were scared and all that, but I wish you had just left me alone. Because it feels like a huge burden now, carrying Mrs. Stein's memories in me. Also, I want you to know that she isn't exactly why I turned my parents in. I mean, she's there, and I can feel her, but she isn't me. I still get to decide how to react. You see? I'm at the controls. And I'm still mad at you, and I think I'm right."

I was really glad this wasn't in-person. I couldn't even look at her hologram in the eye.

"But, anyway, I just wanted to tell you I don't think you are a weapon," she continued. "I think it's more about what you do that defines what you are, not what is inside of you, making you tick." She paused and forced a smile. "See? You're not messed up because of your heart." She said it like she'd found another reason to hate me. I wished I'd implanted more of Mrs. Stein into her, then felt guilty for it.

Her face returned to being all serious. "I'm going away now. Maybe I'll see you again someday. But there's one last thing I wanted to tell you about my mind, besides Nava and the missing person list, and hearing that song." I sat on the bed at her feet. Her recording continued to look at the wall. "It's that sometimes I'm not sure how I'm going to go on from here. But there's a quote that keeps bouncing around in my head. There was a rabbi who once said, 'What is hateful to you, do not do to your fellow.' I think that's about it."

Then the hologram ended, and my room was empty.

Mateo had worn black linen pants and a white shirt with a zipper. He was folding button-down shirts with really showy geometric prints and putting them onto shelves when I walked in.

"Obie!" he said when he saw me. "Can you believe people used to pay for this ugly stuff?" The one customer who'd been browsing looked over at him, shook her head and left. "Oh no, I'm failing at this job already," Mateo said to me. I laughed and we hugged. "Jonas is in the back," he said. I started to protest but he cut me off. "Come on, *amiga*, I know why you're here. It's okay."

Jonas was sitting with his legs resting on a table and gazing into space. One of his hands was touching his necklace.

"Hey," I said. "Wassup?"

"'Sup?" he answered, smiling. I wasn't sure if that was a question I was supposed to answer. I'd only read the first paragraph of the article I'd found on 2020 slang. Jonas took his legs off the table, and I sat there instead. "I just got lunch. It's . . . special."

"Uh-oh," I joked.

"Don't worry. I didn't know if you liked meat on your pizza, so I bought ice cream."

"What?"

"Yes; it was the surest thing." He retreated and returned, balancing bowls, spoons, and everything you'd want to make a sundae. "This is my apology for disappearing."

After he spread it all out on the table, I took a bowl and started making a vanilla sundae with caramel sauce and a cookie crumb topping. I checked the labels—a habit from my parents. No grasshoppers were involved in the preparation of my sundae.

"Should we give some to Mateo?" I asked.

"Nah, his fifteen-minute break isn't for another hour," Jonas answered. I giggled.

"This is the most delicious lunch I've ever had," I told him. I was really having fun, sitting here with him, and eating sweets. I felt so relaxed.

"Would you call it genius?" he asked.

"Uber genius. Like, more than organ-printing-in-the-basement genius."

"Speaking of which," Jonas said, "I have a question for you."

"A question? Is it about ice cream?" I asked coyly.

"No, it's about the shop. I wanted to make you an offer."

An offer? For a second, I thought he was going to ask me to move into his store, then I told myself that was nuts.

"I thought we could become business partners in my organ store," Jonas said. "I'd print the organs, and you'd implant them. I could build you a robot. We'd be a full-stop shop."

Remember when I thought that moving into his store was nuts? I missed those days.

"You want me to do what?" I dropped my spoon onto the floor. It didn't matter, my appetite was gone.

"We could call it, 'Jobie' or 'Obas' and bypass the entire organ printing industry with our nimble venture." His face was open and smiling with eagerness. "Think about it! If someone needed help, they'd just come to us."

Whoa.

I felt this tremendous pressure to keep him happy, to say yes and to have a reason to be with him forever. If I agreed, we could be together, we could have more moments like this, eating dessert at odd times of the day and talking. I could picture it clearly and the idea was tempting.

"No," I blurted out.

Jonas looked crushed. He sat back. "No? How about you'll think about it or do it part-time?"

"It's just . . ." I felt as if my own brain was struggling against itself, one part wanting Jonas and his happiness, and one knowing that I could never operate on another person like I had. "How many times can I have someone's organs, or life, in my hands?"

"How about we start at ten times a week and build from there?" Jonas shrugged and raised his eyebrows.

"No!" I felt I needed to stop saying that so strongly, but I couldn't. "Look, if I were a doctor and had a robot and a nurse and a bunch of others to help me . . . And training! Don't forget training."

"But you don't need them. You've done this—and on a brain." Jonas smooshed his ice cream in his bowl. I wasn't sure if he was demonstrating surgery or his frustration with me.

I remembered what my parents had described to me when they told me why they chose my name. It had to do with not playing God, with not playing with human life all by myself.

"Jonas, I don't think so," I said sadly. It wasn't that I would miss the chance to be in business together, it was that I may have missed the chance to be with Jonas. But that was life—my life, and my choice was clear based on my own brain and memories and whatever else was stored up there. I really wanted to keep Jonas smiling and to be with him, but not enough to ignore what I was feeling. Also, I was totally drained and in no shape to do anything new and wild.

"Why not, Obie? We could help so many people. And we could undo the system; we could speed past it!" He was touching the tiny vial with his mom's DNA in it again.

"Jonas, I want to leave organ printing to the health system. I don't think it's a burden I can hold for now. You know? All those people and things that come together to try and make the right decisions. I'd do it with them. When I'm like thirty."

258

Jonas frowned. "I'm so disappointed," he said. "I had this whole idea."

"Look, I did what I had to do to help Mateo, but I'm happy to let organ duty stay with the system for now, even if it's not perfect. I'm not perfect either."

"You're not?" Jonas cracked a smile. "I guess I thought that you were."

"I'm sorry to disappoint you," I said, wondering if this was it, if I'd walk out of there and never see him again. I stood up to leave and picked up my spoon from the floor.

"Obie, don't be sorry," Jonas said, crouching and putting his hand on mine. "Strong feelings can do that. Makes people seem perfect just as they are."

What did he say? If I'd been wearing that fan hat it would have turned on from the heat rising off my face.

He reached into his pocket. "I got you something. Well, I made you something." He pulled out a beautiful, sparkling . . . tiny white egg on a thin chain.

"Oh," I said, leaving out, "It's what I've always wanted! How did you know?!"

"Hang on, hang on," he laughed. "Open it."

He handed me what I now realized was an egg necklace. I noticed a thin gold line going around the middle. I pressed my fingers gently against it and opened the egg in half. Inside was a messy red circle with red lines coming out of it, like many letter V's. It moved a little, like a pulse.

"It's a blood vessel from early-stage cardiac cells," Jonas said. "I grew it from a chicken. I thought you might not like it if I used a human line."

"You made me a blood vessel?"

"Yes, then put it into this synthetic egg to sustain it. Don't worry, it's not going to grow into a chicken or anything."

"Yeah, that would be awkward," I said. "I hate it when chickens grow inside of my jewelry."

"As I thought you would," he said. He took it from me and slipped it over my head.

"Why did you make this for me?" I asked.

"Because it's real," he answered without hesitating. "Just like you. If anyone tells you otherwise, you can look at it beating, and remember."

The beauty of this gesture took my breath away.

"You know I was thinking," Jonas continued, "that we've actually been thinking too much. About what it means to be alive, and what makes you who you are, and how we can change each other, and if there are some things we never want to change at all, not for anyone."

I nodded while fingering the egg and still enjoying the feeling of Jonas putting his arms over my head to give it to me.

"This necklace is simple, Obie. It's life that's the miracle, not the container. I don't think we need to know much else."

For a moment I thought that Jonas sounded like Mrs. Stein. In a way she was living inside us all. And then Jonas kissed me and my beautiful, inartificial heart beat with understanding.

Acknowledgements

I was fortunate to borrow the time and wisdom of multiple experts while researching and writing this book (of course, this is a work of fiction, and any scientific inaccuracies are all my invention). I would like to thank Olga Fedin Goldberg, MD, Clinical Associate Professor of Neurology & Neurological Sciences at Stanford Medicine, and my friend since age fifteen. Who could have predicted that one day I'd thank you in a book? Also, Lisa Giocomo, PhD, Associate Professor of Neurobiology at Stanford, and an authority on cool things in science and beyond. Steven Kern, MD, FACS, Medical Director and Chairman of the Board at North Memorial Maple Grove Ambulatory Surgery Center and a personal supporter since we sat together at a healthcare conference in San Francisco years ago. Lauren Dunning, JD, MPH, Director of the Center for the Future of Aging at Milken Institute, who is not only brilliant but can carry multiple heavy boxes down three flights of stairs. Jennifer Jennings, MD, Neurosurgeon/Clinical Director of the War Related Illness, and Injury Study Center at the Palo Alto VA Medical Center. LitQuake and the UCSF Memory and Aging Center for hosting a 2019 event "On Forgetting: Writers and Scientists on Memory's Other Side." Chabad of UC Berkeley for the course on Jewish medical ethics and Rabbi Dov Greenberg of Stanford Chabad for introducing Maimonides to me and the idea of the dual nature of human beings, both of which I found inspirational in this book.

I'd like to thank my editor, Misty Mount, for her dedicated and wonderful support of this novel. My writing companions Sue McGarry and Emily J. Popper provided their valuable feedback as I was drafting this book. The lovely Glen Park Branch of the San Francisco Public Library, where I wrote many of these pages. Tobias S. Buckell for his Clarion West Writing Workshop session on subverting clichés.

I have been blessed with an amazing family. My beloved parents, Sarah, and Avigdor Haselkorn, have supported me throughout my life and encouraged me to pursue my passions. Ravid Haselkorn-Galatin and Evelyn Howard reviewed my draft manuscript. Tmirah Haselkorn always alleviates any stress with humor.

Of course, I am grateful to my wonderful husband Ronny Krashinsky for his steadfast backing of my creative pursuit—from his willingness to handle dinner, bath, and bed time as I was writing, to reading the entire manuscript whenever our boys, Isaac and Erez, allowed. I love you all dearly and am lucky to have you in my life.

Finally, I would like to mention my friend Dan Berkowitz, of blessed memory, who did not receive a needed lung transplant and died far too young. Sometimes I wonder if the cure for your sickness lay in the minds of the millions who were exterminated in the Holocaust.

Ateret Haselkorn writes fiction and poetry. She is the winner of 2014 Annual Palo Alto Weekly Short Story Contest. Her children's story was published as a finalist in the 2020 "Science Me a Story" contest of the Society of Spanish Researchers in the United Kingdom. Her work has been published in multiple literary and medical journals and can be accessed at AteretHaselkorn.com.

Twitter and Instagram: @AteretHaselkorn

CPSIA information can be obtained
at www.ICGtesting.com
Printed in the USA
JSHW011149191222
35137JS00004B/8

9 781958 901090